The Truth of the Matter is You're Gonna Learn Today

Sharon W. Hall

Michelle,

Thank you for your support!

Love,

Sharon

DEDICATION

This book is dedicated to my grandparents Thaddeus "Joe" and Celestine Anthony.

CONTENTS

Acknowledgments   vii

Introduction

1   Presto Chango   Pg 3

2   Watch Out for The Big Girl   Pg 21

3   Moving On Up   Pg 29

4   Honey Man, Money Man, Funny Man   Pg 37

5   Jail Bird   Pg 53

6   You, Me and He He   Pg 59

7   Tic Tock Biological Clock   Pg 69

8   Ho...Ho...Ho   Pg 75

9   Out To Sea   Pg 85

10   Broke, Busted, and Can't Be Trusted   Pg 89

11   Three The Hard Way   Pg 101

12   Reverend Lee   Pg 123

13   Fake Ass Brother's ID (FBI)   Pg 147

14   Officer But Not a Gentleman   Pg 157

15   Good to Me But Not Good for Me   Pg 161

ACKNOWLEDGMENTS

God, thank you for giving me the strength to endure each storm I faced while writing this book. I give YOU all the praise, honor, and glory. Lastly, thank you God for giving me a forgiving heart because it has been the key to restoring my soul.

Special thanks to my mom, Dr. Barbara J. Wright, for teaching me to keep moving forward even when I didn't think there was anyway that I could push through.

I would like to thank my husband Randy for being my companion, soulmate, best friend, and the love of my life. Thank you for your support and just being my rock when I needed you.

Special thanks to my children Shauntel "Tootie" Bridges, Stephen "Uneek Shreef" Foster for all the pep talks, which helped me stay on track. Also, thanks for taking the time to critique my unfinished chapters; I knew you would keep it real with me. Kiki Foster thanks for helping me with the book title. Special love to Chavi and Valencia my children who I did not give birth to. Thank you to my heart beats aka grandchildren: Téa, Jeremiah, Dominic, and Christopher.

I want to thank, my Irish twin sister, Stephanie Wright Jenkins for always being there for me. Thank you, Anthony "Tony" aka "Shoes" Wright, my brother, for your support. I hope this book will inspire you to write your own.

Big hugs for all my family and friends!

Tamika L Foster of Puzzle Peace Publications, you made this book what it is. Thank you for being a great editor and sounding board.

TRUTH OF THE MATTER IS YOU'RE GONNA LEARN TODAY

INTRODUCTION

Ladies "The Truth of the Matter you're gonna learn Today" is a book of fictional stories based on real life relationships. I know many of us can identify with several of these stories or know someone who has been in similar situations, which are depicted in this book. Most of my girlfriends have been pretty good at steering me away from relationships; especially when I've had my blinders on.

The truth of the matter is none of us are perfect! My question is when we enter a relationship with our eyes wide open and still see obvious signs that we shouldn't continue with the relationship why do we stay? The goal is to learn from our mistakes. I've had to learn to see things for what they were in my relationships. Then I had to learn to forgive before I entered into another relationship. It is so important to receive love when you heart has been mended.

Ladies, no matter what happens learn to forgive and heal. Lastly, remember that.............

#URFABULOUS

Fearless

Admired

Beautiful

Unique

Loving

Optimistic

Unforgettable

Successful

The truth of the matter is.................

Most of us or someone you know has been the "other woman" in a relationship.

The truth of the matter is.................

Most of us or someone you know has entered into relationship that we really don't want to be in, but we need someone to take care of our sexual needs.

The truth of the matter is……………

Most of us or someone you know has entered into relationships because we need someone just to be the band aid that mends our broken heart from the past.

The truth of the matter is……………

Most of us or someone you know have been in a relationship just to get our bills paid.

CHAPTER 1
PRESTO CHANGO

"Abracadabra! Presto chango!" Greer said as she stretched her arms outward and tossed her head backwards. She looked into the full body mirror that leaned against her bedroom wall.

"Nothing," she said as she sighed and dropped her hands to her sides.

When Greer Perkins was a teenager, she always believed that if there was something you didn't like about yourself, then you should change it. She understood that no one was perfect, but she made every attempt at perfection in her life. She wanted to be the perfect person, look perfect, and be in the perfect relationship.

It was unfortunate that for most of her life everyone told her she had a negative attitude but it wasn't her fault. She was an Army brat and her father's assignments forced them to travel across the world every two to three years. Not being able to build and nurture close relationships can take a toll on a teenager and Greer was no exception. Greer was unhappy and it showed in her actions and in her attitude.

"Greer," her mother started, "no one loves or understands you like your family. We understand why you're the way you are, but if you ever want any friends, a good life, or to go anywhere in your life, you're going to have to work on your attitude. If you don't change your attitude now, you will be an ugly and lonely adult. No one will want you, young lady."

"Abracadabra! Hocus Pocus!" Greer said to herself. "I will change. I will not be an ugly and lonely woman."

Unfortunately, Greer took the whole "working on me, self-improvement" to the extreme. Consequently, she started viewing herself as a perfectionist and she wanted the people around her to level up with her.

The Perkins women had excellent genes and were known for making hearts skip beats and Greer was no exception. She was gorgeous.

Greer had beautiful, flawless brown skin; thick, shoulder-length dark brown wavy hair, almond shaped eyes, and perfectly straight teeth. Greer was five-feet, six inches tall, and was shaped like a Coca-Cola bottle. She had long shapely legs, a flat stomach, a firm round behind, and breasts so perky that they would make a Victoria's Secret model want to model in a bathrobe. Unfortunately, she was never satisfied with the way she looked on the inside or the outside. There was one cousin, Leah, who didn't inherit such great genes. Leah was beautiful, but she was obese. She had to deal with the same internal struggles as Greer though. As beautiful as Greer was, she was never satisfied with her body.

Greer wanted men to find her irresistible regardless of race or age so she took steps to ensure that attraction – to include plastic surgery. The perfectly straight teeth were a result of invisible braces. The Coca-Cola shape came natural for her, but was amplified by breast implants, fat removal from her waist and thighs, a butt-lift, and a nose job. All unnecessary actions to make herself look perfect. The only problem was that men were never able to keep up with Greer's need for perfection. She wasn't sure if the problem was them or herself; more than likely, she was the problem.

For a quite some time, Greer was certain that she definitely was not the problem. She knew just from her experiences with men that it was them and not her. Rahmi Ashtanee is a good example. He was her first real boyfriend. Rahmi was fine. He was an Indian who grew up on the west coast and was motivated to be the best of the best. Rahmi was driven and successful and Greer believed he wanted her at his side.

Rahmi was the CEO of his own software design company. The company started in his living room and turned into a modern, architectural, two-story structure on the waterfront. He was raised by a father who taught him the importance of work and a mother. He watched support his father by working just as hard as his father. Rahmi was spoiled and privileged and hard to deal with, but Greer knew he was the kind of man she needed in her life. Someone she knew would take care of her and she wouldn't have to struggle financially.

Though Rahmi had all of these great characteristics, he had some that were terrible as well. Rahmi was rude and unprofessional. A graduate of an ivy league school for both his Bachelors and Masters degrees, Rahmi believed people needed to earn his respect and his time even though they were paying for his services.

It was important to Greer, as his future partner, to let him know how important it was to be courteous and have a working, professional relationship with his customers. She tried to help him understand the importance of leading his company in excellence, but he wouldn't hear it.

Rahmi felt like Greer knew nothing more than his basic business needs and she felt like she was running his business. Greer was handling his accounting, customer service calls, incoming and outgoing correspondence, and even role-played sell pitch scenarios for him. The sex was good, but she needed more. Greer felt like she was doing too much work in this relationship. There was very little reciprocation and she could tell this relationship wasn't going to go any further.

Greer was sitting in the office with Rahmi one day and he tossed a stack of time sheets at her. She looked at the time sheets and had had enough. Greer took a deep breath and went off.

"Rahmi, I am sick and tired of your mess! Your business may be doing well now, but it's going to fail because you do not listen to me! If I wasn't here you wouldn't be able to run this business. You're a software genius, but can you process payroll on your own?! I'll answer that for you. No! You can't!"

Rahmi squinted his eyes in confusion. Greer rolled her eyes, crossed her arms across her chest and sighed. She could feel the lava stewing and brewing in the pit of her belly and anything she felt for him melted away. Greer now saw Rahmi as a sorry excuse for a businessman. She was disgusted.

Greer stared at Rahmi for ten seconds waiting for him to respond. When he didn't, Greer continued to criticize his atrocious sense of work ethic.

"You don't know how to talk to your clients, you take unnecessary shortcuts, and if you don't hire a professional accountant you will be bankrupt in six months. Stop being cheap and manage your business!

Thinking on it, if it wasn't for me, you wouldn't even have a business. I'm tired of rescuing you, Rahmi. You are needy and you don't need a business partner; you need a superwoman."

Greer tapped her four-inch Louis V pumps and glared at Rahmi expecting a reaction, but Rahmi never responded. He didn't bat an eye and it was evident he couldn't have cared less about Greer's opinion of how he managed his business. Greer grabbed her pocketbook and stormed out of Rahmi's office and never looked back. Helpless men were beneath her and she intended to walk right over them.

Kevin was very different from Rahmi. Kevin was the most desired bachelor in Baton Rouge. He was confident, self-sufficient, kind, and down to earth. He and Greer met at Carnival in Panama and Greer was smitten. She'd had a few bad experiences with guys so as soon as she was able, she looked up as much information on Kevin as possible. She researched all his social media accounts, looked him up on the inmate website, and looked for him on the sex offender registry. She was concerned he that was an overgrown teenager in the body of a grown man that's still trying to be a rapper, but all she got from her searches was how much he loved music.

Greer enjoyed spending time with Kevin while they were at Carnival. They danced and partied together for five days. She was used to partying and dancing with many men, but Kevin was different. She wanted to spend all of her time with him and the time they spent together was amazing.

During Greer's last night in Panama, Kevin invited her to dinner, and she accepted happily. Greer wasn't expecting to seriously date anyone while in Panama, so she had to go out and buy a dress for the evening. She bought a multi-colored halter-top sundress and tan sandals. She purchased a sheer wrap to give the illusion of modesty, but in all actuality, she wanted to be admired by him. Kevin picked Greer up and they went to a local outdoor restaurant. She had never experienced something so exotic and she really appreciated Kevin's attempt at making the night special.

Kevin and Greer talked about their careers and their families for most of the night.

"So, what do you love most about your job," Greer asked.

Kevin giggled and replied. "There aren't a lot of people that love their job. Most people don't even like their job. I'm grateful that I get paid for what I love doing."

"That's great. I don't love my job, but I love what I do," Greer answered.

As they continued to talk, Greer learned that Kevin was very close to his family. His sister and his mother lived in Florida but missed Panama dearly.

"Tell me about your family," Greer said.

"My sister goes to Florida State and she's majoring in Communications. It's just like my little sister to want to talk for a living," Kevin said with a laugh.

Greer and Kevin shared a laugh.

"What does she want to be?" Greer asked.

"A journalist. She wants to be a news reporter and eventually become an anchor for a major station. I keep telling her that reporters will be obsolete one day but she wants to go for it anyway. I'm proud of her," he said lovingly.

Greer just watched him. She recognized that Kevin seemed to have taken on the role as head of the house since his dad was killed in a car accident when he was a child.

Greer and Kevin ended the evening by the water. They laughed and joked all evening. At one point he stared at her as though he wanted to undress her with his eyes. Greer noticed the look and she was thinking the same thing, but she knew it wasn't the right time. She stared at him while she traced the side of her own earlobe to distract her true thoughts of Kevin. Greer was very happy that Kevin didn't try anything because she may not have had the strength to resist him. He took her back to hotel and they exchanged telephone numbers.

"Give me a call anytime you're in Baton Rouge. Call, text, send a smoke signal," Kevin laughed. "Just don't forget about me, Greer," he said and walked away.

"I definitely won't forget about you, Mr. Kevin, and I most certainly will call you when I'm in town."

Greer found herself thinking of Kevin continuously when she returned home. There was something special about Kevin. He seemed genuine and rather mystique. Greer liked that about him. She felt like she made a good impression on him since she didn't sleep with him while she was in Panama.

Greer decided to wait a month before contacting Kevin. It was important to her that he didn't see her as one of those thirsty females. Turns out he was the thirsty one. Kevin called and called and called. He was determined to get Greer to Baton Rouge. After some deep thought she finally agreed. His offer to pay for the airline ticket and the cost of the hotel didn't hurt either.

"When do you want me to come visit?" Greer asked.

"As soon as possible," Kevin said.

Greer was silent for a moment.

"How about next week," Kevin said.

Greer giggled. "Ok," she said.

"I booked your flight while you were thinking," Kevin said.

Kevin gave her the details of the flight. "I'm excited to see you," he said. "I'll be at the airport next week at three o'clock in the afternoon."

"Ok," Greer said. She couldn't stop smiling.

The following week Kevin picked up Greer from the airport.

"Hey pretty lady," he said and kissed her on the cheek.

"Hey yourself," she said.

Kevin dropped Greer off at the W Hotel in New Orleans. She checked in and put her bags down in the bedroom. She walked out onto the patio, closed her eyes, and inhaled the New Orleans air. Kevin watched her take in the atmosphere and decided to wait until she turned around to say anything to her. Greer loved the scenic views from her room. She was excited to spend time with Kevin, but was amazed by this hotel. She turned around and leaned against the railing.

"This hotel is beautiful, thank you," she said to him.

Kevin smiled. "You're welcome," he said as he smiled at her. "I'll be back at five o'clock to take you to dinner. After dinner we can check out a few of the night clubs."

"No problem," she said. "I'll be ready."

Greer showered and dressed in a cute sundress and comfortable strappy sandals. She left the room at four fifty-five in the evening and met Kevin in the lobby.

"You look beautiful," he said.

"Thank you," Greer answered with a smile.

Kevin took Greer to Emeril's restaurant, NOLA. The atmosphere was exquisite and equally romantic. Everything about the restaurant was perfect. Kevin and Greer ordered their meals and continued to talk about his life in Louisiana until their food was brought to them.

The waitress arrived with their food. Greer removed her napkin from the table and placed it on her lap. The waitress placed the plates on the table and asked if they needed anything further, and then left them to their meals.

This wasn't their first meal together, but it's possible that she overlooked the fact that Kevin had no table manners. He never put his napkin in his lap and he held his knife and fork like a savage. He clenched the fork, stabbed the steak, and shoveled the food into his mouth. Greer was a little disgusted, but again allowed the great conversation to overshadow his barbaric table behaviors. They enjoyed themselves so much that time got away from them.

"Look at the time," Kevin said. "We need to get back to change clothes. I'll drop you off at the hotel and pick you up in an hour and a half. Does that work for you?"

"Yeah, that's cool," Greer said

Greer and Kevin pulled up to a club called Masquerade. The line looked like it was wrapped around the building.

"We'll be in line all night," Greer said to him.

Kevin smiled and grabbed Greer by the hand like a child crossing a busy intersection. He walked to the front of the line and approached a guy with "Security" emblazoned on the front of his tight-fitting shirt.

"Mike, this is Greer," Kevin said as he introduced them.

Mike reached out and shook Greer's hand.

"How is it inside?" Kevin asked.

Mike smiled. "It's a full house, man. All of your equipment is already set up," Mike said.

Kevin gave Mike a fist bump and said, "Thanks, bruh."

The club was packed. Kevin had a small table and chair set up near the booth so Greer could be close to him while he was working. Kevin, also known as DJ K-Love, brought the walls down! Greer danced all night. Kevin loved that she enjoyed his music.

After the show, Kevin took Greer to his house. He wanted to introduce her into his world of music as well as into his home. They talked and listened to music for hours.

"I'm in Kevin Heaven," she said.

Kevin laughed.

"You remember that movie, Brown Sugar? It was about the best friends who loved music and..."

"Of course I remember that movie!" he interrupted. "I loved that movie! What about it?"

"I feel like that's us," she said nervously, "Sid and Dre, that's you and me."

Kevin smiled. "Musically in sync," he said.

Greer smiled.

"I'll be right back," Kevin said.

He returned with some squeeze cheese, crackers, and grape Kool-Aid.

Greer broke out into laughter.

"Where on earth did you find squeeze cheese?" she asked as she continued to laugh.

"Look, stop hating on my squeeze cheese!" he said in laughter.

Greer and Kevin continued on with their eighty's music marathon. He ended it with the song *Real Love* by Lakeside.

"That was great," Greer said as she stood up and yawned. "That was one of my favorite songs!"

Kevin stood up and reached for Greer's hand. Kevin walked towards his bedroom and Greer followed him willingly.

Kevin was popular everywhere. Greer felt like she had been with a celebrity. Kevin was the star of the show last night at the club and was equally popular at church. They attended Mass the next day and it was nothing like what she expected. Everyone knew Kevin and seemed to want his attention. Greer watched as he interacted with people and she couldn't help but focus on the cotton mouth and dried spit that gathered in the corners of his lips.

"Yuck," Greer thought to herself.

The more time Greer spent with Kevin the more she realized that his idiosyncrasies drove her crazy. The cotton mouth was almost unbearable. She also noticed that he occasionally stuttered which confused her because he was so confident. He told her he took a public speaking class to help with the stutter, but that didn't seem to work. His wardrobe was outdated. He wore a lot of oversized button-up, plaid shirts and he always seemed to wear tan pants. Greer felt like he should be in a retirement home instead of a DJ booth.

Greer continued to think about Kevin after her plane landed back in Georgia. She thought about how they stayed in bed for the rest of the afternoon before her flight home. With all of his flaws, Kevin was perfect in bed. He was the perfect blend of passion and kinky and Greer loved it. She pouted all the way home; Greer missed him. She texted him as soon as she exited the plane.

She smiled and hit send. "Hey, I made it home safely. Thank you for a beautiful weekend."

"No problem... I really enjoyed myself too," he responded without hesitation. "Next time you come to Baton Rouge I want to take you to my mother's place. I think you will like her cooking. It's out of this world," he answered.

Three months had passed, and Greer had already visited Baton Rouge ten times. Life with Kevin was amazing. Greer loved being around him and his family. Kevin had been the DJ at celebrity parties; and even did the after-party for the Essence Music Festival. Greer spent many days and nights getting lost in movie soundtracks and the different genres of music with Kevin.

Kevin orchestrated a family reunion of sorts. He had his mother flown in from Florida just to meet Greer. His sister had exams and wasn't able to attend, but it was important for his mother to finally meet her. Kevin's mother, Ms. Markland, cooked dinner and dessert for the occasion to meet Greer.

"That was delicious, Ms. Markland!" Greer said.

"Thank you, dear, I'm glad you liked it," she said with a grateful smile.

"Are you ready dessert?" Kevin asked.

"Oh no," Greer said and placed her hand on her stuffed belly. "I don't think I could another bite."

"You have to try just one bite of mom's King Cake," Kevin said. He was determined to get Greer to taste and see just how great a baker his mother was.

"King Cake? Yes! But just one bite. I've never been the one to find that darn baby. Maybe today is my day!" she said with excitement.

Ms. Markland bought the King Cake to the table and set it down in front of Greer and she was amazed. The cake was purple, gold, and green and was adorned with tiny golds beads.

"Ms. Markland, this cake is beautiful!"

"Thank you, dear. Here, Kevin. Let Greer have the first slice," she said.

Ms. Markland smiled and handed the spatula to Kevin.

Kevin sliced a large piece of the cake and placed it on a small plate in front of Greer.

"Kevin! That is too big!"

Kevin laughed. "You don't have to eat the whole thing, just try it."

Greer's fork hit something hard on the first try and her face lit up.

"I found the baby!" she yelled.

Greer lifted her fork and a diamond ring came up with it. Greer didn't move; she was in shock. Kevin's mother stood, unsuccessfully, holding back her tears. Kevin removed the ring from her fork and licked off the cake and purple icing. Greer couldn't move. She was still in shock. Kevin's mother now had tears streaming down her face. Kevin smiled lovingly at Greer as he wiped the ring off with a napkin. Kevin stood in front of Greer and dropped to one knee.

"Greer Perkins, will you marry me?"

Greer broke into tears. Kevin remained on his knee with the ring in his hand.

"Greer, will you be my wife?"

Through her tears, she finally answered, "Yes! Yes, Kevin! Yes, I'll marry you!"

Greer jumped from the seat and wrapped her arms around Kevin's neck and they fell to the floor in laughter. Kevin managed to break free from her loving grip and placed the ring on her finger. Greer was still in shock, but she was ecstatic.

Greer and Kevin discussed the wedding's location. It made sense to them to go to Las Vegas and make it big and memorable, but they couldn't agree on it at that time. Kevin could sense that something was bothering Greer but waited until they arrived at the hotel to ask about it. Greer took a long shower and Kevin waited lovingly and patiently for her.

Greer walked out of the bathroom. Kevin was sitting on the bed smiling until he saw her face.

"What's the matter, baby?"

Without hesitation Greer answered, "Kevin, I want to talk to you about some things."

"Ok. What's up?" he asked.

Kevin stood up and walked over to Greer. He led her over to the sofa and they sat down.

"What's that in your hand?" he asked.

"I wrote this list while I was in the bathroom," she answered.

"A list of your bridal party and wedding guests?" he asked with a laugh.

Greer ignored him as she unfolded the paper and cleared her throat.

"This is a list of some improvements you need to make before we're married."

Kevin laughed, but Greer figured it was an emotional response. He didn't respond so Greer proceeded to read her list.

"Kevin, for starters, you need to learn table manners. You are supposed to put your napkin in your lap before you eat in case food falls from your fork. There is a correct way to hold a knife and fork and you are not supposed to stab your food like an axe murderer in a sorority house. You need to see a speech therapist to assist with that stutter. I can help you with subscribing to magazines to help you with your wardrobe upgrade," she said.

"My clothes? You don't like my clothes?" he interrupted.

"Please let me finish," Greer said sternly. "You need to upgrade your wardrobe. You dress like you're going on a cruise for senior citizens. There is a glob of dried up spit that gathers in the corners of your mouth when you talk for long periods of time. I'm thinking it may be helpful for you to periodically look in a mirror to catch it before it forms. If we're going to be married, I think it's important that we're honest with each other so if anything else comes up that I think is a problem I'll let you know," she finished.

Greer felt like a weight was lifted off her chest. She took a deep breath and smiled at Kevin. Kevin stared at Greer blankly. He sat up then stared at the ground as he reflected on his life.

"Greer..." he started.

"Oh yeah, I just remembered one more thing. You can't be a DJ for the rest of your life. Like, I understand it as a hobby, but it can't be your full-time job when you have a family you have to take care of. Ok, now I'm done," she said with a genuine smile.

Greer now recognized that Kevin was upset.

"What's the matter, baby?" she asked him.

"You want to reinvent me before we get married," he stated.

"Oh no..." Greer started.

"I'm not asking you a question, Greer. I'm telling you that's what you're trying to do. It was selfish, childish, and egotistical of you to come up with a list of things I need to fix. Trust me, I know I have things to work on, but who are you to create a list detailing my flaws. When did you become a life-coach? Do you think you don't have flaws? Because we all have flaws, Greer, including you. Furthermore, if I do decide to marry you after this, I can see you coming up with a new addition to the list every week."

Kevin stood up and started pacing the floor with his hands in his pockets. Greer watched him and wondered what he was thinking.

"If I do decide to marry you," she thought about the words Kevin used. "He said if," she said to herself.

Greer knew Kevin was upset, but these things had to be said. She had to tell him the truth.

Kevin stopped at the window and turned to face Greer. He addressed her calmly, but sternly.

"What happened to you in your life that you have to be so critical of me? I'm not perfect, but neither are you. Do you think you can just wave your critical little magic wand and *presto chango*, everyone's flaws are fixed to suit you? If you can't accept me the way I am, this relationship is over."

Greer stared at him. She thought he was trippin' and couldn't possibly be serious. She watched his whole demeanor change. He went from calm to frustrated and his eyes were fixed on Greer.

"Do you have anything to say, Greer?"

Greer shrugged her shoulders like a spoiled ten-year old child. Kevin nodded his head acknowledging her lack of response.

"Greer, I love you, but I'm not going to marry someone who feels the need to constantly criticize me and others. It's evident I will never be good enough for you. It's over."

Kevin picked up his keys from the table and walked out of the hotel room.

Greer sat on the sofa in confusion. Kevin's words cut deep.

"I don't understand," she said out loud. "All he had to do was make some minor changes! It's not like I asked him to have reconstructive surgery or anything! What did I say wrong?! Everyone can stand to make some self-improvements. I'm hurt he even took it so personally. I'll call him in a week so or," she said as she got into bed and pulled the comforter to her neck, "he'll be alright."

Greer went back home and she never heard from Kevin. Every time the phone rang or she received a text message she hoped it was him, but it wasn't.

"Why isn't he checking on me?" she wondered.

After about a week, Greer called Kevin, but he didn't answer. She called every day for five days and still no answer. She left voice messages and sent text messages, but she never heard from him. Greer became worried so she called her cousin, Demi, for advice.

"Hey Greer," Demi answered.

"Hey girl. You have a minute? I need some advice."

"Sure, what's up?"

"Can I come over?" Greer asked.

"Sure, I can't wait to hear all about him and whatever went down," Demi said with a giggle.

"How'd you know something was going on?"

"You only call me with relationship issues and for NBA All-Star game tickets and that's not until February so clearly it's about a relationship," she giggled again.

Greer drove and picked up a bottle of wine to take to Demi's house. Before reaching the register, she decided it might be a two-bottle kind of conversation so she picked up another bottle of rose´ wine. Greer arrived at Demi's and they made themselves comfortable on the living room sofa.

Greer told Demi all about the situation with Kevin. She told her everything from the moment they met to the King Cake proposal. Demi listened calmly as she sipped her wine.

"Cuz," Demi said as she took a sip from her oversized wine glass, "what exactly did you do?"

"Why do you think it was me?!" she asked defensively.

Demi laughed and put her hand to her chest to help her swallow her wine. "Greer, go ahead with your heartbreak story. And for the record, I know you so that's why I know you did something."

"Demi, you know I love Kevin with all of my heart and soul. He proposed and I said yes. I had never been so excited in my life," Greer explained.

"Get to it, Greer. You don't need to defend yourself to me. What did you say to him?" Demi pushed.

Greer took a deep breath. "I only told him about some areas in his life where he could make some improvements. I felt like it was important to tell him before we got married. Isn't marriage about being vulnerable and honest? Well, I was! I was kind of afraid to tell him, but at least I told him the truth!"

"Greer," Demi said.

"Ok, ok, ok," Greer said as she pulled out the list.

Demi's eyes widened.

"This is what I said to him," Greer said and she read the list to Demi. Demi looked at Greer in sadness and with disbelief.

"Did you really say those things to him?" she asked seriously.

Greer was silent as she folded the paper up and put it into her purse.

"Greer, please tell me you did not say those petty and insignificant things to him! I would have broken off the engagement too! Kevin probably expects that the criticism will never end," Demi said.

"He said that," Greer said as she took a sip of her wine. "Demi, do you think I believe I'm perfect?"

"Yes!" she yelled out. "Greer, our mothers have really messed us up! They convinced us that we could always improve something with ourselves. Fix this, tuck that, say this, don't say that. Greer, you took this whole self-improvement thing way too far."

Greer thought about what Demi said for a moment and nodded in agreement. "You're right, Demi."

"You will never be able to stay in a relationship at the rate you're going. Greer, listen to me. THERE IS NO MR. PERFECT! None of us are perfect, including you and its time someone told you that. You really need to see someone; a therapist maybe, because your need to be perfect and expecting it from others is unrealistic."

"I will. Thanks for listening to me, Demi. Do you think I search for the imperfections in others so I will feel perfect myself?"

"I don't know, Greer, but I do know that if you get some help you're going to be just fine."

Greer returned home and laid in her bed. She reached into her nightstand drawer and retrieved her Bible.

"I don't even know where to start," Greer said to herself as she held the Bible on her lap. "Lord, please help me. I'm not a bad person. Please tell me what I need to do."

Greer decided to open the Bible and let it fall on a random page. It opened to Ephesians, chapter four. Verse number twenty-nine was at the top of the page so she just started reading.

"Do not let any unwholesome talk come out of your mouths, but only what is helpful for building others up according to their needs that it may benefit those who listen."

Greer had tears in her eyes. She couldn't read any more, but also recognized that she wasn't supposed to. The message she needed at that time she received in that one verse.

"God," Greer prayed, "I'm sorry. Please forgive me for constantly hurting people with my words. As a kid we were told that sticks and stones could break our bones, but words would never hurt, but that's a lie. The bruises of sticks and stones go away, but the wounds of words can stick with us forever."

Greer cried herself to sleep that night. She woke up the next morning and knew she needed to make a change in her life. She made an appointment with a Christian therapist and started seeing her three times a week. The therapist was very helpful. She helped Greer get clarification on her situation and understand her need for perfection.

Greer started attending a local church and weekly Bible study. One day in Bible Study, the teacher talked about a scripture that Greer would never forget: Psalm one-thirty-nine, verses thirteen and fourteen. "For You created my inmost being. You knit me together in my mother's womb. I praise You because I am fearfully and wonderfully made. Your works are wonderful, I know that full well." It helped Greer to remember that she is an imperfect person, but she is wonderfully made by God, just like all His children, including Kevin.

After one month of intensive therapy, Greer called Kevin, but he didn't answer the phone. She had come to accept that she missed out on the best man of her life and she had to live with that. Greer was sad, but she knew that she would be different if she was given another chance with Kevin or any other guy she met.

Greer's mother had been calling her every day since her break-up from Kevin. Their relationship had gotten better. Greer's mother started going with her to church and they were both growing spiritually. They spent less time criticizing one another and more time enjoying each other's company and Greer loved it.

"Let's go out to dinner," Ms. Perkins suggested, "my treat."

"Ok. Where do you want to go?"

"How about Ruth Chris Steakhouse?" her mother suggested.

"Sounds great!" Greer said.

Greer and her mother ate until they were absolutely stuffed. They even ordered dessert, chocolate cake and apple pie ala mode. For the first time, neither of them was concerned about weight gain, sugar pimples, or anything else that could come from overeating the way they did that night. Dessert was taking forever to get to the table. Greer started to pray to keep from getting annoyed.

The waiter was headed towards their table.

"Finally, thank God," Greer said out loud.

The waiter looked way too familiar. Greer squinted and to her surprise, she realized that it was Kevin. He was carrying their dessert. Kevin arrived at the table and Greer started crying.

Kevin smiled and put the tray down on the table. "Hey Greer! How are you?" he asked.

Greer couldn't control herself. "Excuse me," she said and ran to the restroom to compose herself. She ran to the bathroom and allowed her tears to fall. She blew her nose, wiped her eyes, then freshened up her make-up.

"God, are you listening right now? Is this my second chance? If so, I promise I won't mess this up. Please bring Kevin back to me. Amen."

Greer left the restroom and went back to the table where Kevin was sitting with her mother.

Greer smiled as she approached the table. Kevin's smile disappeared and Greer became nervous.

"Maybe he thought I went to the restroom to write another list," she thought to herself.

"Have a seat," he said.

Greer sat down nervously and interlocked her fingers on her lap. Kevin sat beside Greer and put his hands-on top of her hands.

"Greer those things you said the night I broke off our engagement really hurt me. After talking to my mother, she told me that maybe your mother could offer some insight. Thankfully, I spoke to your mother after the two of you had started going to church together so she was able to be honest about her own personal issues and how they impacted your life," he said.

Greer's tears fell slowly as she listened to Kevin.

"I loved you enough to try to figure it all out, Greer. Your mother told me about your growth and your newfound relationship with Christ. She told me about of how God has done wonders in your life. I knew in order for Him to restore You; you had to be willing to allow Him to do so according to His will. You needed to be influenced by Him and not by me. I would have accepted you regardless of the things you were dealing with. You needed God to help you understand yourself better and how to make changes in your life."

Greer was in shock. She was blown away by Kevin's words, but more so that her mother planned the entire thing. Greer was happy. For the first time in her life, she felt like everything was perfect.

Kevin took a deep breath and dropped to one knee. Greer's tears dropped from her eyes once again.

"Greer, the last time I did this my mother was there. This time, I knew it would be great if your mother was here. Greer Perkins, flaws and all, will you marry me?

Greer stood up and screamed, "Yes!"

Kevin and Greer were married a month later in Jamaica. Both of their families and close friends attended the beautiful, beachside ceremony. Greer was happy to become Mrs. Kevin Markland, but even happier to be a child of God. She was glad that God had accepted her the way she was created, flaws and all.

CHAPTER 2
WATCH OUT FOR THE BIG GIRL

"Take a number." That's the response I give'em. The men who stare and drool as I strut all two-hundred and sixty pounds of my five-foot-seven inches of sexiness down the street.

I was a thick chick as a teenager. My self-esteem was tattered and my shape was round so I could never imagine the type of attention I'm now receiving.

"Watch out for the big girl," they sing as I seductively toss my tail in these strappy sandals.

Yes, you'd better watch out, because I'm not taking prisoners, just your man.

Let me tell you a little about me. It's obvious you're wondering. I'm used to it, so that's ok, but this confidence has a root. It may not be deep yet, but it's getting there. My name is Leah Perkins and I'm a confident and curvaceous, 25-year-old thick chick. Believe it or not, the men love me. I hate my thick, course hair, but I know how to rock a wig and make it look like my own.

I have always been on the tall side, but I didn't pick up the weight until about the sixth grade. My mother, who has never weighed more than one-hundred thirty pounds, always complained about my weight and compared me to my itty-bitty cousins. Instead of helping to build my self-esteem, she beat it into the floor. It got worse when I returned home from college. Instead of the fabled "Freshman 15" my mom asked if I gained the "Freshman 50." I knew I needed to lose weight for health reasons, but I was never motivated enough to do anything more than arm curl more food to my mouth.

All of the women in my family are small with flattering figures. That gene passed me by, but it didn't stop me from being great. I won singing competitions in high school and in college. I also modeled in local fashion shows when they wanted to highlight the plus-sized women. That gene, however, didn't skip Greer. Greer was beautiful. She had this short bob that framed her narrow face. Greer had smooth brown skin, almond shaped eyes, a big beautiful smile, and a Coke-bottle figure. My mother would always compare me to Greer and it drove me crazy!

"Why can't you be more like Greer?" She'd ask.

"Why don't you wear your hair like Greer?"

"Why don't you try doing your make-up like Greer?"

Greer was a sweetheart and she would do anything for me but being compared to her constantly made me resent her in a way. I can admit that I was jealous and that jealousy got the best of me at times.

Now before I tell you all of my business, I want you to know that I do not need your judgment. I get enough of it from my mother. Now, I love Greer with all of my heart, but as my self-confidence increased, so did my sex drive. So, it only made sense that I sleep with the men mama thought I couldn't have – Greer's ex-boyfriends. Like I said – I don't need your judgment. I had four of them in a regular rotation. They liked her looks, but they loved my passion. One experience with me and they were hooked. They never took me out on actual dates, but I didn't care. I was content just to spend time in their arms and in their beds.

My mother's boyfriend, Mr. Royal, used to feel sorry for me. I don't know if its because they tried to make me feel bad about my weight or not, but you could see the pity in his eyes. One day, while I was home on spring break, Mr. Royal saw me standing around flirting with a few guys. I watched him shake his head and walk back into the house. After exchanging numbers with the guys, I went back into the house to the disapproving eyes of Mr. Royal.

"Let me tell you a story, Leah," he started.

Mr. Royal told me the story about the ugly duckling that grew to be a beautiful swan. It helped my confidence, but it also made me wish I was prettier and thinner than Greer and my other cousins. Mr. Royal was nice to me; nicer than mama even. There were times when I would go months without hearing an encouraging word, but each time they came they were from him.

"Let's go for a walk," he said.

I wasn't really excited about the walk until Mr. Royal told me we were going to Lincoln Park. I picked up my pace at the thought of the men I could pick up there. Mr. Royal almost had to run to keep up with me.

We arrived at the park a few blocks later. Mr. Royal was almost out of breath, but he called my name.

"Hey Leah, look over there," he said.

I looked over and saw an ugly duck – the baby swan. Then he pointed to the adult swan. I had heard that story several times in my life, but seeing the swans together made it so much more real. I was sad and amazed at the same time. Tears ran down my face. Mr. Royal hugged me tightly then wiped my tears. His hand brushed against my breast and he immediately apologized. It felt different, probably because he was old, but I liked it.

"It's ok. You can touch both of them if you want," I said to him.

He was clearly shocked, but didn't say anything. Mr. Royal turned to leave the park and I followed closely behind him. We walked home in silence.

The next morning, I felt terrible. I never usually feel bad about things I say to men, but I did with Mr. Royal. When I got downstairs, my mother was leaving the house for work and Mr. Royal was sitting in the kitchen. I walked over to the dog to feed him and prepare to walk him and I spoke to Mr. Royal.

"Morning."

He didn't respond. I put water in the dog's bowl and turned to get his food from the pantry and Mr. Royal was standing right behind me. Without a word, he grabbed my waist with his left hand and my breast with his right hand and put his tongue in my mouth. I was scared and turned on at the same time as he grabbed my hair, pulled up my skirt, and pulled my panties down. After that morning, Mr. Royal and I had sex two to three times a week.

My mother was clueless. Every time she commented on my weight, I had sex with Mr. Royal.

"I may be a big girl, but I'm rocking your man's world," I would say to myself.

I overheard her talking on the telephone telling one of her friends that he was slipping in bed; it wasn't as good as it used to be. He was slipping with her because he was putting all of his energy into me. She also mentioned he wasn't paying bills like he used to. He started giving me gifts, but I'm not sure why he stopped paying bills. Either way, mama was done with him and since she was, I was too. She told Mr. Royal to pack his things and leave and he did. Would you believe he thought we'd still be seeing each other? I was only doing it to hurt mama so I was done with his old behind. On to my next conquest. I think I need a bigger challenge.

A few months had passed, but no real challenges were presented. Then I heard it. Mama was talking on the phone and she yelled out, "Oh my goodness! Demi is getting married!" Demi is another one of my Coke-bottle figured cousins. She was just as beautiful as Greer, but she was light skinned with a big butt and perfect teeth. She wasn't as nice to me as Greer so I wouldn't have any problems at all taking her man. This was the challenge I needed. It's easy to get a guy in bed – especially if he has a woman who's not taking care of him. It's a real challenge when he's engaged to your beautiful cousin. This should be fun.

I knew I had to play this just right. I had slept with ninety percent of Greer's ex-boyfriends so I knew what they liked, but I had never been with any of Demi's boyfriends because she didn't live close by. I had to play this just right. The challenge was getting the new guy alone long enough to take him.

"Demi is bringing her fiancé over for dinner," mama announced.

"We're going to make it a family dinner since he's coming in from out of town..."

"Bingo!" I'll get him when they come over for dinner.

"What's his name, mama?"

"Brock. He and Demi hooked up in college. He's in medical school now. With her becoming a pharmacist they're going to make real good money. See, you should have gone to school with Demi. Then maybe you would have yourself a good man..."

I tuned her out once the comparisons started. School was back in session in a few days. I didn't have a lot of time to work my "Big Girl" magic on him. Time to put this plan into action.

It was great to see the family. I was a little uncomfortable though. I wasn't too bothered being the biggest in the room, that was normal, but I remembered how some of them made negative comments about my weight and my choice of school, my major. Everything. It was a rare day, if ever, that anyone in my family said anything positive to me. My family was cruel at times and as much as I tried to fight it, the pain always found its way back to the surface.

Brock looked much better in person. The Facebook and Instagram photos were outdated. He was taller than I thought. The social media photos showed him with a mustache only, but he now had a mustache and a full beard. It was evident that he worked out because his muscles bulged slightly through his shirt. Brock had clearly grown up since his last photo post. I couldn't wait to lure him into my bed.

The family sat around playing cards and taking shots of Goldschlager. I kept my eye on Brock in hopes of noticing when he became tipsy enough to tempt. After seeing Brock throw back two more shots, I decided to make my move. Brock was unphased. I went to the restroom and adjusted my cleavage. I figured maybe he needed more of an incentive. I touched up my make-up and sashayed out of the bathroom towards him. I chatted him up about medical school while trying to give him the eye, but he still wasn't biting. I brushed passed him closely while allowing my behind to slide against his manly part, but he still didn't respond. It was Demi. He was focused on Demi. After a while they were gone. I searched the house for them then heard noises coming from the bathroom. They were in there getting it on. Clearly my curves gave him an appetite. There's no way he could walk away from all of this!

The next morning, Brock and Demi came over for brunch. This was their farewell meal before heading back to school. Demi was in the kitchen preparing food with mama and asked if I could give Brock a ride to the store for the ingredients he needed for his famous pancakes.

"No problem. I'll bring him right back," I said with a devilish grin.

Brock quickly purchased his items and returned to the car. I drove off slowing making small talk.

"Brock, how long have you and Demi been together?"

"Almost two years," he replied proudly. "I planned to propose in front of your family, but I couldn't wait. I did it just before we came here."

"That's sweet," I said as I drove behind a building and put the car in park.

"Why are we stopping?" he asked.

I got straight to the point. "Why don't you let me suck you off before we get back. Just our little secret," I said as I reached to unbutton his pants.

Brock was appalled.

"Are you crazy?! I love Demi! I'm engaged to your cousin!"

I couldn't believe he was turning all of this down. I rolled my eyes, put the car in drive and we drove back in silence. Brock looked like a scared puppy.

Brock was visibly shaken when he walked into the house. Demi pressed for him to tell her what was wrong, but he kept saying he was fine. Brock was weak so I knew he wouldn't say anything. He didn't want to stir up mess in the family he was trying to be a part of.

Demi started crying and Brock gave in. I was scared. Not because they would find out, but because I knew this was going to get ugly quickly. Demi gave me the look of death. I could see both anger and disappointment in her face at the same time.

"Is this true?!" she yelled.

I rolled my eyes, stood up, and held my ground. "Demi, grow up," I said calmly with an attitude. "I've slept with many men. I slept with all of Greer's ex-boyfriends. I even slept with Mr. Royal. Brock is just another guy."

The room was silent. I don't think the Perkins family had ever been this quiet. Everyone looked at me with pity except for mama. She looked at me in a way I'd never seen in her face before.

"You disgust me. You are disgusting," she said as she walked towards me. "This is why you don't have a man now. You are fat, lazy, and disgusting," mama said with a twisted face.

"You don't have a man either, mama," I snapped back. "I was able to give him something that you couldn't and..."

Before I could utter another word, my face was stinging. Mama had slapped me. Shocked, I grabbed my things and left the house without a word.

I drove around for hours before I finally stopped. I sat in the car in silence. I looked in the mirror to see if my face had a hand print and for the first time I actually saw myself. It was as if mama had literally slapped some sense into me. I was sad. I cried as I thought about the chaos I had created in my family. I looked up to wipe my tears and realized I was sitting beside a Christian-based counseling facility. I walked inside and told the lady at the desk that I needed help. Over time, a therapist helped me to address my low self-esteem, the pain I carried around, and the destructive behaviors I had been displaying.

I wanted my family to forgive me, but I was afraid to face them. For years I was numb, but now I was starting to feel again and it was terrifying. My therapist sat with me as I reached out to mama, Greer, and Demi. They agreed to come to support group sessions and though everything wasn't fixed at the first few meetings, they eventually forgave me.

I learned a lot in my sessions. What was important, though, is that I come from a family of strong and forgiving women. Most important, I learned that I am wonderfully made – even at my size, loved, and valued by God.

CHAPTER 3
MOVING ON UP

"Summer, summer, summer time... ooh summer time. Time to sit back and unwind." This is my jam! DJ Jazzy Jeff and The Fresh Prince did their thing with this song! My favorite season had arrived. Though it may have made better sense to be outside in the warmth of the summer sun, I had the perfect view of all the action and the cool breeze of my oscillating fan right from my bedroom window. I also had a perfect view of Camden Project's finest men in all of their sweaty glory. From sunup to sun down, the basketball court was the meeting ground for everybody who was anybody. The only body I had my eye on was Smitty Wilson.

I loved my view and my hood but every teenaged girl between the ages of 16-18 had an exit plan to escape it one day. There were three exit plans that we all pretty much agreed on, but they weren't always guaranteed. You could get a boyfriend with a good job, but there weren't a lot of them because they were taken already by the girl that was bold enough to get his attention first. The next best thing was to get yourself a drug dealer. That wasn't hard, but if a deal went bad, they could get killed and you'd be left with nothing. Some of us tried modeling and singing, but nothing ever really worked out.

Smitty was my plan A, B, C, and Z. First of all, he was fine as hell. He was six-feet tall with an athletic build. He had pearly white teeth and wore a gold crown with an Ace of Spades carved into it. Smitty was sharp. He always sported the latest designer clothes and he wore thick gold chains. Smitty wasn't just any drug dealer, he was a rich drug dealer and he was going to get me out of Camden Projects.

Now don't get me wrong, I may have wanted to leave, but I loved my hood. There were all types of fun places to hang out and get lost in the midst of the summer. The neighborhood laundromat, Suds-N-Stuff, was the gossip hotspot. Last summer, the owner installed a stereo system in the laundromat. We would go there to wash and fold and dance to pass the time. We'd start the laundry and next thing we knew we'd be ready to fold. And we didn't just go there for laundry and gossip, but now we had a daytime dance spot. If we happened to walk by and our jam was on, we would go inside and dance around in the folding area. There was also a corner store, Pop's, where we would go in and talk to the cuties behind the register. They worked in Camden, but they lived in the suburbs. We felt like they were out of our league so we didn't even try. One of my favorite places was Tony's. Tony's was the pizza parlor that was owned by a Black man. People would joke that no Black man could make pizza like the Italians, but Mr. Tony put his foot in those slices! So, as you can see, Camden had its places of greatness. These were good times in Camden, but I still wanted out.

In came Smitty with his fine self. Smitty gave me butterflies in my belly. When I looked at him my heart would skip a beat. Smitty was twenty-two years old, and with me being seventeen, I felt like I didn't even exist in his world. I knew I would have to play up my attributes to get his attention. At five feet, seven inches tall, I was worth taking notice of. I had what most people described as "good hair" because it was naturally long, straight, and it was jet black. My fair skin was accentuated by my dark eyebrows, full eye lashes, and full lips. While I was beautiful, I also had a cute, bubble booty and perky breasts. I know that's what's expected at my age, but I wore my looks much better than some of the other females my age. In my mind, I was "modelish." What I lacked in height and talent, I made up for in looks.

No matter how much fun I had, I knew I was not destined to live in these projects for the rest of my life. My aunt Lucille told me that I should marry a man with money. She knew best because she hit the jackpot when she married Chuck Washington, the neighborhood postman. Everybody knew that you had some money if you worked for the post office. Chuck moved her out of the projects and bought her a beautiful, three-bedroom house on the westside. I had hoped that if I played my cards well enough Smitty and I would be married and buy a house in her neighborhood. I'd be far enough away from the projects, but close enough that I could visit if I wanted to.

It was officially time to execute my "get out of the hood" plan. I wasn't getting any younger and I didn't want any of these other females trying to take Smitty. I figured I would try two plans at once. The word on the street was Rod 45 was the man I needed to contact for a modeling portfolio. Rod 45 was well connected. He knew models, agents, the best agencies, and local music producers. I knew I couldn't sing, so I went with the modeling route.

I had learned from Toya, my best friend, that Rod 45 did a photo shoot for Tinka Willis.

"Toya, who is that?" I asked.

"You know Tinka," she started, "the one we called 'Tinka Stinka'."

I cracked up laughing. "Oh, you mean that girl that smelled like a bad piece of fish?"

"Yes, her!" she answered with a laugh.

Toya went on to say that the portfolio done by Rod 45 landed Tinka a job at New Beginnings Modeling Agency. Hell, I figured if he could help her funky tail get a modeling job, then I knew I could be the next top runway diva. I called Rod 45 and set up an appointment for five o'clock in the evening on the next day. He asked me to meet him at Pop's convenience store. I figured he must rent space in the back of the store to do the photo shoots.

Rod 45 looked very different from what I imagined. He was short; maybe four-feet, eleven inches and he was overweight. His Tupac shirt was too small, and his jeans were too big. He wore dirty Air Force Ones and they looked too big. Rod 45 wore two rings on each finger and a gold cap on one of his front teeth. On top of all of that, his breath smelled like he'd just eaten a fresh shit sandwich. I was not expecting this at all. A man with all of these connections and this type of clout had no sense of fashion or hygiene. He kept smiling at me, but I was not interested or impressed. It was borderline depressing. I was nice to him, though. Besides, I knew he and Smitty were good friends and I was hoping he would share my pictures with him. You know… kill two birds with one stone.

I entered the space we were using for the photo shoot and was instantly pissed off. There were canned goods and boxes all over the place.

"Are we doing a shoot for a grocery store?!" I asked myself.

"How you doing?" he asked just before he asked for the thirty-dollar session fee.

"I'm ok," I said with a fake smile.

"My fees are going to increase after today," he said, "because my shoots have helped five girls get modeling contracts with Homegirl Model Management."

I immediately dismissed his terrible outfit and breath and became excited about the possibility of signing with a modeling agency.

"You're really pretty," he said to me.

"Thank you," I answered.

"Change into your bikini," he said as he was setting up.

"Change where?" I asked looking around.

"Behind the Campbell Soup pallet," he said, not really paying me any attention.

I wasn't too bothered because the pallet was tall enough to give me privacy. Besides, at four-eleven, I'm sure he couldn't see over the pallet. I was a little bothered by the atmosphere, but what could I expect for thirty dollars? I couldn't really be choosy.

"Come on sweet thing," Rod 45 said, "I don't have all day."

I came from behind the pallet and the bright lights sent me into a daydream of a Victoria Secret runway show. I walked out behind Tyra Banks wearing my Angel wings, white high-heeled shoes, silver rhinestone bra and matching bikini panties. I made it to the end of the runway and struck a sexy pose for the camera. My daydream came to a screeching halt when I heard Rod 45 banging the camera on a crate in front of himself.

"Dammit," he said in an agitated tone. "Now I have to use my back-up camera."

I put on my oversized shirt until he was ready.

"Ok, let's go again," he said.

I removed my shirt and started posing. The light from the camera was bright. I almost couldn't see Rod 45's face, but I could clearly see that big-bellied munchkin was using a disposable camera.

"What the hell?" I thought to myself.

Rod 45 took about ten photos and he was done.

"That's it?" I asked myself. "We're done?" I asked him.

"Yeah, I think we got enough," he answered.

"Ok, so what next?"

"I'm going to send the film off to be developed and I will get back with you," he said.

An hour later Rod 45 called me. I was not expecting to hear from him so quickly. When I saw the photos, I understood why. I was so mad! The pictures looked terrible! It looked like someone took a bunch of amateur pictures in the basement of a grocery store. Oh wait... that's exactly what had happened!

"What agency is going to take me seriously with these photos?" I asked him.

"What? These are good pictures!"

He said that like he really believed it! To make matters worse, that was my last thirty dollars. I had to babysit this bad behind boy for two weeks to earn that money. How in the world was I going to earn more money without babysitting? It was like my whole world was turned upside down. That big-bellied munchkin took advantage of me and I missed the deadline to submit my pictures to Homegirl Model Management. That was such a setback in my plans. Now what?

I went home and sat in the window. Watching the neighborhood cuties through my window usually brightened up my day, but I was devastated. I sat on my bed and cried. I laid down and held my pillow to my belly wondering how I was going to get the hell out of these projects. I started thinking about plan B, Smitty, and I drifted off to sleep.

I had this wonderful dream that Smitty and I were a couple. He came over to take me out for my birthday. He showed up with a gift-wrapped box and a dozen of mixed flowers. Anyone could buy roses from the gas station, but Smitty was different. He was classy. I put the flowers in some water and sat on the sofa to open my gift.

"What could be in a box like this?" I wondered.

I started crying when I opened the box. He bought me the rabbit fur jacket I saw in Morton's department store a few weeks back.

"You like it?" he asked.

"I love it," I said as I tried it on. "It fits perfectly."

Smitty flashed those perfect white teeth and I gave him a "thank you" kiss.

He had me put the jacket on so I could wear it to the next birthday surprise, which I figured out was dinner when we pulled up to Big Maw's barbeque spot. It was freezing in there so I had to keep my jacket on.

"I have one more surprise for you," he started.

"What more could you possibly have for me?" I asked.

Smitty ran out to the car and returned with a cylinder case. I couldn't imagine what could be inside. He opened the case and pulled out plans to a house he was having built from the ground.

"Is this a house?" I asked. I wanted to be sure before I got too excited.

"This isn't just A house; it's OUR house," he emphasized.

I was crying all over again. I couldn't wait to tell Aunt Lucille my good news.

We finished our dinner and as I got up, I realized my jacket was shedding all over the place. The girls sitting behind us were laughing so hard that they were crying. I rolled my eyes and kept walking.

"My jacket may be shedding, but I have a man who loves me and is having a house built just for me," I said to myself.

I woke up to the sound of gunshots. I got to the floor and stayed low until I heard the sound of sirens near the courtyard. I heard people yelling, screaming, and crying. When I finally got the nerve to look out of the window, I saw two ambulances and several police cars.

I went downstairs to find out what was going on when I ran into my friend Wanda.

"What happened, Wanda?"

"Girl, somebody just killed Smitty," she said.

I felt like my future was completely ruined. First the photo shoot and now Smitty. How was I going to get out of here?

I stayed in my room a lot over the next few weeks. My mother was a bit concerned, but I always told her I was fine. Smitty's death wasn't hard on me because I had lost my ticket out of the hood but because it made me take a good look at myself. I had to make my own way out of Camden Projects. I took inventory of my skills and my self-worth. I had always been smart and hard working. I don't know when it happened, but I got caught up in what my friends and my family thought was "success." Having a boo at my side was nice, but I didn't need a man to succeed. I graduated high school a year early and with honors. Thinking back on it, my family didn't attend my graduation. They had their own vision of what my life should look like, but I no longer agreed with that picture.

My mother wanted me to go into business with Rod 45. For what? He had multiple businesses to include a beauty salon, a barbershop, and his terrible photography business, but he didn't want to leave the hood. He didn't have any goals. I later learned that Rod 45 tried to persuade my mother to talk to me because he wanted to marry me. Yuck! He was unattractive and I didn't even know him like that. My mother wanted me to marry him so that our family could have money to move out of the projects, but now I knew that I could do that on my own.

I enrolled in college and wasn't really surprised that I was accepted. I was surprised that I finished so quickly. I had my own plan and this plan had me on the fast track of life. After college I moved to Kentucky and attended the University of Kentucky Law School. None of my family attended my college or law school graduations. At this point I didn't even expect them to attend.

The sky was the limit. I was offered a lucrative position at a large firm in Atlanta, Georgia almost immediately after law school. I passed the bar and purchased my first home. Who would have thought that little Ms. Chloe Francis from Camden Projects would not only become an attorney, but be a home owner? I was almost as shocked as others would have been, but I recognized greatness in myself and ran after it.

I was happy and I was enjoying my life, but I was sad at the same time. My mother was disappointed with me. With all of my success, she couldn't understand why I wanted to leave the projects. She said she wanted to leave. I even offered her to come live with me, but she refused to talk to me. I called her several times between college, law school, and the move to Atlanta, but she wouldn't take my calls.

I missed my mother and I even missed Camden at times, but I didn't miss that seventeen-year-old girl that changed clothes behind a soup pallet and had dreams of marrying a drug dealer.

"She was a mess," I think to myself with a giggle as I stare out the window of my living room.

I learned a lot in Camden Projects. The most important lesson I learned was to know my self-worth, love myself, and not to depend on a man to take care of me.

CHAPTER 4
HONEY MAN, MONEY MAN, FUNNY MAN

I want to say that my life is difficult, but it isn't. I'm young, beautiful, and educated. As you could expect, my parents are pretty good looking as well. My daddy is very handsome. I have always wanted a man with my daddy's looks so we could have beautiful children. I know that sounds shallow, but at least I'm honest with myself. Unfortunately, I'm not as close to him as I used to be since he and his wife moved out of the state. I really miss my daddy.

I learned the hard way about some things in life. For example, my daddy was married when I was born. Not married to my mother – he had a wife named Connie. Connie was pretty, but she wasn't as pretty as my mom. My half-sister, Raquel, and I are six months apart. Our brother, Roy, is five years younger than us. I don't know why it took me so long to figure out the closeness of our ages. I guess I really didn't care when I was growing up. The conflict, for lack of a better word, is undeniable now.

Connie is still very nice to me considering I'm the result of her husband's affair. I used to think she was going to poison me when she would cook dinner, but I survived. Oftentimes I went home hungry because I refused to eat her cooking.

My mom is single now; well kind of. She's not married, but she has "friends." Every time I think about her not being married, I wonder what happened. All of my guy friends in high school always joked about wanting to sleep with her. Thinking back on it, they probably weren't joking. That just pissed me off.

Mom had three men in her life that I really liked and hoped would be my step-dad. She always broke up with them before that would happen though. After a while I just stopped hoping.

I used to ask my mom why the relationships didn't work. There was always some reason that seemed kind of petty so I just stopped asking after a while. One day I came in from school and she was in the midst of a break-up. I walked past them like I didn't hear or see anything. I went up to my room, laid across my bed and starting writing in my journal. A while later, my mother came in and leaned against my desk.

"You'll be graduating soon and heading out on your own," she said.

I turned and sat up to give her my undivided attention.

"I think it's time we had this conversation," she said.

"I already know about sex mom," I said as I rolled my eyes.

"This isn't just about sex," she said as she lit a cigarette. "It's about life. It's about money. It's about character," she said as she flicked her cigarette ash into a cup on my desk.

"Money and character? What are you talking about, mom?"

"The man you choose needs to have plenty of money, he needs to be funny, and give you plenty of honey."

"Mom..." I started.

"Listen, Rhonda," she started. "Its hard to find one man with all of those qualities. Always be open and listen for where you can use them in your life. The money man pays the bills. The funny man makes you laugh no matter what's going on in your life, and the honey man gets your body," she said directly.

"Mom!" I yelled.

"Rhonda, you're eighteen years old. Grow up! You're old enough to hear this. When you leave this house, I need to make sure you can take care of yourself and you won't be able to if you don't have this information," she said as she took a long pull on the cigarette. "Hell, you should be taking notes."

I listened to everything she said and determined that's why she never got married. I get it. Why sit and wait on one man when you can have a variety? I think I'm going to enjoy the variety. She seems like she did. We live in a nice house. I get whatever I ask for and I don't have to work. I wear nice clothes. It works for her. It has to work for me.

I enlisted in the Air Force immediately after graduating high school. I scored really high on the entry exam so I had my choice of where I wanted to go. I can't lie, I chose the cyber technology field so I could meet rich men, for job security, and make a lot of money in case I had a hard time finding a money man.

After completing all of my Air Force training, I was assigned to Joint Base Andrews in Maryland. The DC, Maryland, and Virginia area, better known as the DMV area, was great for jobs and socializing, but the ratio of men to women was awful. Dating in the DMV area was going to be challenging, but interesting to say the least.

I called my mom to tell her about the potential dating challenges and to get some advice when she told me that her "friend" Mr. Goldstein had died of a heart attack. I was sadder than expected. Surprisingly, mom didn't seem sad at all. Mom had dated him for eight years and I liked him better than her other friends.

"Let me know the details of the funeral," I said.

"I sure will," she said and we ended the call.

About two weeks had passed before I realized that she never mentioned it. I called her to see what was going on.

"Hey, did you forget to give me the details of Mr. Goldstein's funeral?"

"No. The funeral was last Thursday," she said calmly.

"Mom are you serious!?" I was livid. Mr. Goldstein bought my first car, gave me money every time he saw me, and treated my mother like a queen. "How can you be so calm?!"

She remained quiet.

"Mom!" I shouted.

"Rhonda," she sighed. I could tell she was smoking a cigarette. "I have to go," and she ended the call.

I held my phone in complete shock. I looked up the obituary online after I calmed down. I figured I would send a sympathy card to the family. There was a nice picture of him online. He was handsome for an older man. I continued to read looking for a next of kin and learned that Mr. Goldstein had been married for thirty-five years!

I called mom back immediately. I tried to calm myself while the phone was ringing.

"What, Rhonda," she answered.

"Why didn't you tell me Mr. Goldstein was married?" I asked.

"I didn't think it mattered," she answered calmly.

"It didn't matter?" I asked confused.

"Rhonda, did you forget about our conversation that quickly? Mr. Goldstein was my money man. I cared about him, but I kept him around for money. You're not supposed to get attached to any of them. You use them for what you need and you move on to the next when you lose one."

"I guess I understand," I said to her.

Mom sighed.

"What are you thinking?" I asked her.

"Rhonda to be perfectly honest with you, all of my boyfriends were married. Your dad was my funny man and Calabrese was my honey man. Every man in my life has a specific role. Sometimes the roles change depending on your needs. Like I told you before, every woman needs a money man, a funny man, and a honey man.

"I'm not judging you, mom, it just caught me off guard. You're never afraid to get hurt?"

"Not at all. Not emotionally anyway. You have to know yourself and know when to walk away."

Mom and I talked for a little while longer then she ended the call.

I laid in bed that night and realized that mom really gave me the perfect way to handle my relationship options. I fell asleep and woke up excited about the new possibilities of dating in the DMV area.

A few weeks later and I saw an officer that had been pursuing me for quite some time. He was stationed at Joint Base Andrews, but he traveled frequently. Dr. Terry Sinese was the Officer in Charge of the base medical clinic. He had a pretty smile, but that was about it. His body was decent for an older guy, but I wasn't certain I could make him my money man. I knew I had to have sex with the money man and I wasn't physically attracted to him.

"Hello, Doctor," I said in a flirtatious tone.

He caught it. "Hello pretty lady. How are you?"

"I'm well, thanks for asking. How about yourself?" I asked with a smile.

"I'm great now that I get to see that pretty smile of yours," he replied.

I smiled. He smiled back at me.

"Got him," I thought to myself.

Terry and I started seeing each other regularly. He was married with three teenaged children, but I didn't care. He was my money man and my only expectation was that he contributed to my finances. Terry bought me gifts regularly. A few months after we started dating, he bought me a diamond tennis bracelet. After a few more months he was paying my rent, taking me on shopping excursions, and putting up to two-thousand dollars in my pocket. His requirements were reasonable. He wanted sex a few times a month and discretion. He wasn't too bad looking after a couple of thousand hit my account so he was easy to tolerate. I knew at some point I had to find me a funny man and a honey man so discretion and not spending too much time together worked just fine for me.

Nolan Cross is arguably the funniest guy I've ever dated. He's cute, but in a teddy bear sort of way. Every time I think about how we met it makes me laugh.

I was shopping in Pentagon City, courtesy of Dr. Terry, when I met Nolan. He was on his lunch break and boldly struck up a conversation with me.

"Hey girl!" he called out.

I turned around to see this 30-something year old man wearing a Metro subway jacket. I didn't respond.

"I know you hear me talking to you. Girl I can see you in my future!" he jokingly yelled out.

I couldn't help but bust out laughing.

"Ha!" he said. "I finally got a laugh." Nolan smiled and showed off small, pearly white teeth. "You are beautiful," he said seriously.

"Why thank you," I answered.

From that moment he tried to talk me to death. Ordinarily, I ignore strangers, but he had such a wonderful personality, and he was too

41

funny for words.

"My train is coming. It was nice meeting you, Nolan."

"If I give you my number will you call me?" he asked.

I was shocked so I didn't answer immediately.

"Come on now," he said. "Don't make me waste this napkin and ink by writing down my number and you're not going to call."

I laughed again. "Ok, yes, I'll call you," I giggled.

Nolan handed me his number as the train pulled up.

"You enjoy the rest of your day beautiful," he said.

I turned and smiled at him as I boarded. "I think I just met my funny man," I thought to myself as I found a seat on the train.

Nolan was the perfect gentleman. Having him as the funny man was easy. He never tried anything so I didn't feel obligated to have sex with him or even kiss him. In all of our conversations I learned that he writes poetry, had an amazing singing voice, and he was a natural comedian. I liked Nolan. He wasn't about games or foolishness. He just wanted someone nice to settle down with and make them laugh. I wasn't ready to settle down, but I definitely was always ready for the laughs. I enjoyed hanging out with Nolan, but laughing didn't pay the bills. It was time to get back to Terry so my funds didn't dry up.

Terry had finally let his guard down. I was accompanying him on business trips when possible and he was now depositing five-thousand dollars into my bank account every month. If he was spending money like this on me, I wondered how he spoiled his wife. After one trip and sleeping with him a few times I determined that his wife was filling her time and their bed with a younger man who knew how to put in that sexual time. I must have forgotten to mention that Terry was a one-minute man. It was often I had to please myself after he left my place. Terry was weak in bed, but his money was long and strong.

Terry and Nolan were both trying to get my time, but my body was in need of a honey man. I wasn't satisfied by Terry and Nolan had never made a move. A woman has needs and I needed to some honey to go with my funny and my money. Mom was right.

I joined a gym in hopes of meeting a different caliber of man as well as maintaining my figure. I was on the stair climber listening to music when this fine specimen covered in sweat and muscles walked past the machine.

"Have mercy," I whispered as I slowed down on the stepper. He was wearing tank top with the gym's logo so I assumed he was one of their trainers.

"How do I get him to approach me?" I wondered.

I had been going to the gym for almost two weeks before he noticed me. Here I was wearing my sexiest workout gear when all I had to do was act as if I didn't know how to use a machine properly.

"You're going to hurt yourself," he said with a slight smile.

"Really? I always do it this way," I said.

"I'm surprised you haven't already hurt yourself," he said with a laugh and adjusted the machine. "By the way, I'm Jefferson."

"I'm Rhonda," I said with a smile.

I watched as he demonstrated how to use the machine and gave me a few pointers.

"Thank you so much," I said.

"So, what are you trying to accomplish?" he asked as he flirtatiously glanced at me from head to toe.

"I'm trying to get my beach body back," I said.

"Doesn't look like you've ever lost it," he replied. "I'm a physical trainer. I know a fit body when I see one."

"Well thank you," I replied with a smile.

Jefferson had agreed to personally training me three days a week. I was interested, but I had to play hard to get. I saw the other women in the gym throwing themselves at him so I knew I had to go a different route.

Weeks had passed and Jefferson couldn't figure me out. Some days I would flirt; other days I would be all business. Jefferson was intrigued.

"We should go out," he said bluntly as we walked around the vitamin store after one of our training sessions.

"Go out where?" I asked nonchalantly.

He smiled. "Let's go get a salad."

I looked at him with the side eye.

"Oh, I'm sorry. Your husband must be home waiting for you," he said.

"I'm not married, but I do have things to do," I said.

Jefferson handed me his business card. "Give me a call some time. I think we have a lot in common."

"I will," I said as we walked to the cash register to check out. Jefferson walked me to my car and opened my door.

"So will I hear from you tonight?" he asked.

He shut my car door and I rolled down the window. I smiled.

"Is that a yes?" he asked.

I rolled up my window and pulled out of the parking space. I stored his name in my phone at the first stop light and thought to myself. "I can stop being so hard towards him now. I want some of that honey."

I slacked off on the gym for a little while to get back to Terry. He was becoming restless. He had been wanting to see more of me, but I couldn't stop thinking about Jefferson. We planned a date that night and it was just like every other night. The only difference was during his three-minute moment on top of me I imagined it was Jefferson.

"That was great baby," he said as he rolled to the other side of the bed.

Terry was snoring minutes later, but I needed him to leave. I had a date with Nolan. I hopped out of the bed and showered before I woke him up.

I shook him, "Terry, wake up."

"What's the matter?" he said like he had been sleep for hours.

"I just got a call from the office. We may have a cyber threat. I need to go in."

Terry got up, dressed, and left my townhouse. The plan worked beautifully.

I put on a cute little outfit then left to meet Nolan. We sat and talked about his last two shows in Virginia Beach and North Carolina. He talked about upcoming shows in Pennsylvania and New Jersey as we sipped expressos and ate cookies. That reminded me that I need to get back to the gym to see Jefferson. After that miserable episode with Terry, my body was aching for Jefferson and we hadn't even kissed yet.

Nolan and I ended the evening at Underground Comedy in D.C. It was his surprise for me. Nolan excused himself from the table and was taking quite a while. I busied myself on social media while waiting for him to return. The lights dimmed and the announcer called his name. I was pleasantly surprised! He told me we were going to see an up and coming comedian and it turned out he was talking about himself. I laughed the entire time!

Nolan and I walked around and chatted for a while before we ended the night.

"I really like you, Rhonda," he said with a smile as he turned to face me.

"Awww... I like you too, No..." and Nolan leaned forward and slid his warm tongue into my mouth.

I wasn't expecting that at all, but damn it was nice! After that kiss, I wondered if Nolan could serve a dual role as the honey man and the funny man.

I went to the gym a couple of days later. Still playing hard to get, but not so much, I casually walked past Jefferson in my hot pink and black leggings and matching sports-bra top.

"Hey," I said.

"Hey yourself, beautiful. How are you?" he asked.

"I'm doing great. How about yourself?" I asked.

"The gym has been packed. I think everyone is preparing for summer vacations," he said with a slight laugh. "I figured since I hadn't seen you that you were traveling."

"Oh no," she started, "I've just been working a lot. I'm back, though, and ready to work it out!"

"I like your enthusiasm," he said checking me out. "Abs?" he asked.

"Full body," I said flirtatiously.

Jefferson smiled. "Give me about twenty minutes. Let me finish with another client."

Jefferson took about forty-five minutes, but I busied myself with the stair climber and the treadmill.

"You started without me," he said in a disappointed tone.

"Cardio is just my foreplay," I teased. "I'm ready for the real thing now."

Jefferson smiled.

"Let's hit the weight room," he said.

I followed him closely and could smell the sweat mixed with his cologne. He led me to a machine that works by abs and he touched by back and abs to show me the proper position. My body almost went limp. The sexual attraction was intense.

Jefferson looked me in my eyes as I laid on the machine with my knees up. He felt it too.

We moved to another machine and I caught him eyeing my breasts.

Jefferson spotted me as I did a few sets of bench presses. He let me struggle on the last set before I realized he was doing it on purpose.

"You want me?" he asked.

"Yes," I managed to get out.

Jefferson grabbed with weight from me with one hand.

"Your help..." I breathed out.

"What?" he asked.

"You asked if I wanted you. I wanted your help," I said with a smile.

Jefferson smiled. "Let me cook you dinner."

"When?"

"Tonight. Six o'clock," he said directly.

Damn this man is sexy. "Ok."

I hate being late, but I arrived a few minutes after six o'clock so he didn't think I was desperate. I fixed my hair and rang the doorbell. Jefferson opened the door.

"Damn," he whispered.

"Mission accomplished," I said as I walked in uninvited.

His cologne invaded my nostrils. He shut the door and told me to make myself at home. I almost got naked with that invitation.

"Thank you," I said.

We ate dinner and had great conversation. We talked about our childhoods, our parents, our dreams, and how he got into personal training and other casual topics. Jefferson allowed the melodious voices of The Commodores to fill the air. I leaned my head back for a moment, but opened them because I could sense his presence near me. Jefferson pressed his lips against mine. Two songs later, Jefferson and I were in his bedroom.

"Dear God, let this last longer than three minutes!" I shouted in my mind as he undressed me.

His body was sexier than I imagined. He used every muscle in his body to please me. I can't remember the last time a man loved me to sleep. We had just finished and I couldn't wait until the next time.

I woke up in Jefferson's arms. I tried to move to use the bathroom, but he squeezed me closer. I giggled.

"I have to use the bathroom."

He released me and watched me walk to the bathroom. Jefferson was stretching in front of the window when I returned.

"I like our chemistry, Rhonda. I'm really feeling you."

I couldn't help but smile. "Are you really?"

"I am," he smiled back.

"I'm feeling you too, Jefferson."

"Show me how much," he said and climbed back into the bed.

I pulled the sheet and met him in the middle of the bed for round two.

I awakened in Jefferson's arms. "Are you asleep?" I asked him.

"No, just enjoying the smell of coconut oil in your hair," he said.

I couldn't help but laugh. "You're so random."

"I know," he said and squeezed me tighter.

"Jefferson."

"What's up?" he answered.

"I want to tell you something," I said seriously.

"Ok, shoot," he said.

I told him about mom encouraging me to have a money man, funny man, and a honey man. He listened quietly as I told him that he was my honey man, but that I liked him and wanted more. I told him that I was ending it with Nolan and Terry and asked him to forgive me.

He remained quiet for a while. I almost thought he fell asleep, but he spoke. "So what's going to change when you leave here tonight?" he asked.

"I'm going to contact them both and end it with them. I just want to be with you, Jefferson."

"Really?" he asked almost as if he didn't believe me.

"Really," I answered and turned to face him.

"So you don't have any feelings for them at all?" he asked without judgement.

"No. I was just trying to do what mom told me. It seemed to work for her so I figured it would work for me."

"Ok," he started, "but from here on out no more secrets. It's just me and you."

"Ok," I said as I buried my face into his muscular arms and squeezed him tightly.

I arrived home and was greeted by flowers from Terry. I put them in water, but wanted to throw them into the trash after my night with Jefferson. I knew if I threw them out, he would ask about them.

I finally looked at my cell phone when I arrived home and realized that Terry called me seventeen times between six o'clock last night and eight o'clock this morning.

"Overkill," I said as I rolled my eyes.

"Hey baby, I'm at your door," the message played. Delete.

"Hey baby, are you home?" Delete.

"Hey baby, she's out for the night and..." Delete.

"Rhonda, where are you? I've..." Delete.

"I pay this damn bill! You better answer this phone!" Delete. Delete. Delete. Delete. Delete.

"Oh boy," she thought to herself. I'm going to have to do a lot of schmoozing to get my next allowance.

"You have one new message," the phone read.

"This better not be another message from Terry."

"Hey Rhonda, its Nolan. I'm back in town and can't stop thinking about that kiss. Give me a call when you're free. Let's go out to dinner."

He was sweet, but I was bored with him. I called him and agreed to a date the following night.

Nolan and I were enjoying the evening when he invited me back to his place.

"For what?" I asked nonchalantly.

"I think its time we take this relationship to another level," he said.

Such a gentleman. It was sweet, but not at all as sexy as Jefferson and it definitely was not going to happen. I needed fire, like Jefferson. Nolan was watered down.

"Nolan, we don't have that kind of relationship."

"I know, but we can," he said as he reached for my hand.

I looked into his eyes and smiled. "Nolan, you are a sweetheart. You are the funniest man I know, but I think we should end this now."

Nolan looked like a hurt school boy.

"Ok, Rhonda. I think I should take you home now."

"Good idea," I replied.

I hadn't seen Terry for almost a month. He stopped paying my bills, but the five-thousand dollars allowance continued.

"Cha-ching" I said to myself every time I received an alert from the bank.

I was able to spend my time with Jefferson and Terry's money on myself. This was perfect. Thanks mom.

Terry's wife had been demanding so much of his time I thought she had found out about us. I didn't care because the deposits kept coming. When Terry finally started calling again, I told him I was busy. I was able to avoid him for three months and collected more than fifteen-thousand dollars in deposits. "Cha-ching!"

I was enjoying my time with Jefferson. I was happy. Jefferson may not have been rich like Terry or even as funny as Nolan, but he was more than just honey. Jefferson was good to me and good for me. My mother told me that I could never find all three in one man, but I found a man – a real man and I was content in that.

I knew I had to break it off with Terry. Honestly, I figured he would just go away and the deposits would stop. Two more months had passed and two more deposits came when Terry finally called me again.

"Hello," I answered.

"Rhonda, we need to meet. May I come over tonight?" he asked politely. Something seemed weird in his voice, but I figured he was upset because he hadn't seen me in months.

"Sure. How about seven o'clock?"

"That works. I'll see you then."

My phone alert sounded. Terry had just made another deposit of five-thousand dollars into my account. For the first time I wasn't excited. I didn't even want it. I was going to give it back to him when he arrived that night.

Terry is here. I'm upstairs writing in this journal, wasting time, and trying to figure out how to end it nicely. I can't seem to come up with a nice way... no nice words. Oh well... here it goes.

Vanessa closed Rhonda's journal and pressed it to her chest.

"This is all my fault!" she screamed. "Oh God! This is all my fault!"

Jefferson ran into Rhonda's bedroom.

"Vanessa!"

Rhonda's mother had slid from the bed and to her knees as she held the journal that told of Rhonda's money man, her funny man, and her honey man. The journal that told of Rhonda's last night alive.

"That crazy bastard killed my baby!" she cried.

Jefferson pulled Vanessa to him and she cried on his shoulder holding on to the journal for dear life.

"Jefferson, this is my fault," she said with tears staining her foundation-covered face.

"It's not your fault, Vanessa. What's that?" he asked motioning towards the journal.

"Vanessa looked at the journal then back at Jefferson. She knew if he knew the truth, he would hate Rhonda so she lied.

"It's just an old diary from high-school I found while going through some of her things. I miss my baby," she said.

"I know, I miss her too," Jefferson said.

"Just leave me. I'm ok," Vanessa said.

Jefferson gave Vanessa a box of Kleenex and left the room.

Vanessa walked around the room looking at pictures of her daughter and she stopped at a picture of her daughter at her Air Force graduation. "My poor baby, she cried. "You weren't supposed to dump the funny man, fall for the honey man, and you definitely were not supposed to be choked to death by the money man! My poor baby!"

Vanessa continued to stare at the photo. "Oh Rhonda, forgive me. I get it now. You can't play with people's feelings... no matter what your needs are."

Jefferson entered the room to check on Vanessa. "You ok?"

Vanessa wiped her tears. "Yes, thank you Jefferson."

He put his arm around her shoulder then escorted her from Rhonda's bedroom.

CHAPTER 5
JAIL BIRD

"Oh my goodness! I overslept!" I said out loud as I jumped out of the bed. I was supposed to be meeting Maxine at the bus station at nine-fifteen in the morning. Here it was eight o'clock and I've still got to shower.

I jumped in the shower, hit my "hot spots", hopped out and was barely dried off before Maxine was calling my phone.

"Hey Tracy! Are you on your way?" she asked.

"Yes," I lied. "I'll be there in ten minutes."

"Ok," Maxine started, "the bus will be here at nine-fifteen and it's already eight-forty."

"Ok," I answered and hung up abruptly. I didn't need any reminders.

I snatched the bonnet off of my head, fluffed my curls, threw my make-up bag into my purse, and ran out of the house.

"Record time!" Maxine shouted with a laugh as I reached the station out of breath.

"Girl, I overslept," I said while trying to catch my breath.

It was nine-twelve when I looked at my watch.

The bus arrived on time and left on time. Thank goodness because that was the only bus leaving for the Jessup Correctional Institution that day.

I still can't believe I'm headed up to this prison to visit a man. I never imagined falling for a convict, but when I met Calvin Barron, better known as Big Cal, it was love at first sight. Big Cal was tall and had dark chocolate skin. He had dark features: thick black eye brows, dark low-cut hair, and deep set, dark brown eyes. His body was solid. It was obvious that he spent most of his time lifting weights. His arms, abs, and back muscles were well-defined. I remember staring at him. I stared at his feet and by the time I made it to his eyes, he was staring back at me.

Big Cal and I met about four months ago at the prison. We, the lovely ladies of Purdue Farms, volunteered to drop off Christian books to the inmates to increase their morale. The guys were always glad to see us. They affectionately called us the "Chicken Chicks."

We were able to sit with the inmates and have discussions about the books. Big Cal and I always ended up together talking about the books he chose. When it was time for us to partner up, he and I chose each other.

I made sure I dressed extra cute and smelled extra sweet every time I went to visit. My knees would get weak and I had butterflies in my stomach every time I saw him. It was love at first sight.

The monthly visits from the Chicken Chicks became weekly visits between me and Calvin. Big Cal became my friend. We talked about our lives, our friends, and life in general. Calvin shared with me that he was in prison for the attempted murder of his girlfriend. He told me of how they had always had a rough relationship, but he never tried to kill her. I was mad when he told me that story. I think she hit him and he hit her back in self-defense, but I don't believe he tried to kill her. Some females are so dramatic. You know how some of us can be – always trying to keep a good man down.

Cal didn't have any family. His mother had died a few years earlier and he never knew his father. Big Cal needed me and I was glad to be there for him. I couldn't really afford it, but I put forty dollars on his books every two weeks. He needed someone to look out for him.

Calvin and I talked for hours during our visits. He was very attentive. He could always tell when I changed my hair, changed perfumes, and wore new outfits to see him. I was head over heels!

Cal became friendly with some of the guards there and they would give him special privileges. Some would let us hold hands. One correction officer, in particular, Officer Moe, would turn his head away from us to allow us to sneak kisses and intimate touches. I looked forward to Officer Moe guarding. I knew that was orgasm day. Big Cal would touch me oh so softly and in just the right place. I always went home with a smile, but it was bigger when Officer Moe was on duty.

There was one CO that I couldn't stand, Pat Logan. The inmates called her Fat Pat. She didn't like me at all. She rolled her eyes at me every time I was there. At first, I thought she didn't like me because she was jealous that I looked better and she thought was a dime piece – a perfect ten, but I later realized she had a thing for Big Cal. She would cut our visits short, make side comments, and noises during our visits. She drove us crazy!

I wasn't worried about her because Calvin and I had something real. I knew Fat Pat didn't have a chance. Every time I saw her, she looked like she was gaining weight. I understood where her name came from. About a month or two later, she was wearing a maternity uniform.

"Good for her," I thought to myself. "Now she can stop trying to block me and Calvin. She's such a hater."

I heard from Maxine that some of the COs were sleeping with the inmates. I trusted Calvin, though, so I wasn't worried at all. Our relationship was on lock.

Everything was going great. Calvin and I were exchanging letters, reading books, and spending time together on the weekend visits. We were discussing moving our relationship forward and starting a family. We were in love. Everything was perfect until I was laid off from the plant.

I was nervous when I went to see my boo. Not only did I have to tell him that I was laid off, but I also had to tell him that I couldn't put money on his books.

"Hey baby," I said as I greeted him in the visitor's room.

"Hey," he said.

Big Cal stood up and smiled as he reached down and hugged me.

"God, I love this man," I thought to myself.

I told him the news and he was very comforting.

"I'm sorry to hear that baby. We'll be alright, though. I still got some money on the books."

I had been laid off, but I was still happy thanks to Calvin.

I'd had some money saved up so even though I couldn't give Big Cal any money for his books, I was still able to visit. I was so pleased with the way Cal had handled my news of being laid off I went out and bought a cute, but inexpensive, new outfit to impress him.

I arrived at the bus stop on time this time. It wasn't a "Chicken

Chick" weekend so Maxine wasn't there to keep my company on the bus.

The atmosphere at the jail was a little weird when I walked in for the visitor check-in. Moe was on duty.

"Hey Moe, what's up?" I asked.

"Nothing for you, Tracy," he started. "Your boy is in solitary confinement for twenty-nine more days," he said.

"Solitary? Twenty-nine days?! What are you talking about? What happened!?" I asked as I slammed my wristlet on the counter.

"There was a brawl in the yard. He started the whole thing," Moe said with a sly smile.

"Brawl? What was he fighting about?" I asked.

Fat Pat shot a look at me and started laughing. I rolled my eyes.

"Moe, what was the fight about?" I repeated.

"I don't know," Moe answered with a laugh. "Nobody would talk. They threw him in yesterday for a thirty-day stint. You can see him in twenty-nine more days."

"You might want to grab that bus before it leaves," Fat Pat said.

I grabbed my wristlet then ran for the bus. I rode home and was very disappointed.

"Twenty-nine days is too long," Tracy thought to herself.

She decided to get another job to pass time and to earn money during the lay-off.

Tracy managed to save eighty dollars and decided to put it on Calvin's books to use when he got out of solitary.

The thirty days seemed to take forever, but Tracy was excited the day had finally arrived! Day thirty fell on a Thursday so Tracy decided to surprise Calvin with a weekday visit instead of waiting for Saturday.

She rode the bus to the jail and arrived at the visitor's center. That weird feeling was present again, but Tracy ignored it.

Fat Pat walked into the visitor's center and stopped abruptly.

"Chicken Chick," she called out to Tracy.

"What, Pat?" Tracy answered.

"He expecting you today?" she said and walked over to Tracy.

"What business is that of yours Fat Pat?" Tracy answered.

Pat laughed. "You're right, its none of my business at all. Let her through!" Pat shouted to the guard.

The gate buzzed loudly, the door slid sideways to open and Tracy entered towards the visitor's lounge.

Tracy entered and looked for Big Cal. Moe spotted her first.

"Tracy!" he said with shock.

"Hey Moe," she said with a confused look on her face. "What's wrong with you?" she asked as she scanned the room for Big Cal.

Before Moe could respond, Tracy spotted Calvin sitting with an unfamiliar White woman.

Fat Pat, who had somehow entered without Tracy's knowledge spoke with a sly grin, "This is going to be good."

Tracy marched over to Calvin and tapped the woman on her shoulder.

"Hello," Tracy said to the woman, "who are you?"

Calvin dropped his head down to the table. The woman looked Tracy up and down before standing to her feet.

"I'm his wife! Who the hell are you?"

"Wife?! Calvin! Is this your wife?!" Tracy asked surprised.

"You don't need to talk to him, you can talk to me! He's big, but he ain't got no power! I run this!"

Calvin's wife cursed me out. I couldn't say anything. I could only hear Fat Pat muffling her laughter in the background.

"I'm sick of Calvin's mess! He's been cheating forever! Now I turn around and this fat bitch is pregnant." His wife motioned to Fat Pat who was rubbing her round belly.

Tracy was dumbfounded.

"This is too much," Tracy said.

"Too much? You're just another side chick! You're not even his type with your run-down Reebok Classics. Do they still even make those? And who does your hair? That wig is easily a year old. Little girl, let it go. Whatever you've been doing to impress his lying ass is foolish. You need to look into a mirror and focus on your appearance. Leave these jail birds alone!" she said.

Fat Pat was now laughing hysterically.

Moe just stood there with a blank look on his face.

Tracy felt like a fool as she rode the bus back home.

"I easily gave that lying bastard five-hundred dollars over the past six months," she thought to herself. "Money I definitely couldn't afford and, according to Calvin's wife, should have spent on myself."

Tracy's self-esteem had taken a hit, but it wasn't broken.

"I was starving for male companionship – attention," she thought to herself. Instead of looking for a relationship, I need to look at myself and not just my hair and shoes, but my heart and my mind. I need to look at what I want for myself in my life. I even have to accept that it may not include a boyfriend at this time. Bottom line, I really just need to focus on me.

CHAPTER 6
YOU, ME AND HE HE

"Come on in, Charlee" the psychotherapist instructed. "How are you feeling today?" she asked.

"The same way I've been feeling for the last six months, Doc," Charlee answered.

"You keep telling me that you will eventually tell me what's going on, yet in six months the only thing you have told me was that your marriage was over, your twins are leaving for college, and your two best friends want to kill your husband."

Charlee remained silent.

"Charlee," Dr. Montgomery, said calmly.

Charlee looked at Dr. Montgomery but said nothing.

"I'm not usually one to throw things around," she started, "but I did that night."

Charlee stood and walked over to the window while Dr. Montgomery sat quietly and waited for her to continue.

"Let me start from the beginning," Charlee said. "My husband, Mateo, and I have been married for twenty-three years." Charlee paused to reflect on the number of years she'd spent with him. She walked back over to the sofa, sat down, and removed her shoes to get comfortable.

Dr. Montgomery smiled.

"You think I'm stalling, don't you, Doc?"

"No, I think you're afraid to be vulnerable," Dr. Montgomery answered.

"You're probably right," Charlee answered.

Charlee was quiet once again. Dr. Montgomery matched her silence.

Charlee sighed and continued. "Long story short, Mateo was my first love. We met at Hampton University in the late eighties. We worked hard and we played hard, but we had goals and we had a plan. The goal was to live life together as successful doctors. After medical school and securing employment at the local hospitals, Mateo and I got married and settled down in Fairfax County, Virginia. We loved each other dearly, but we went to college and medical school together. We didn't want to work together at the same hospitals," Charlee giggled.

Dr. Montgomery giggled with her.

"Anyway, a few years into working at the hospital, I found out I was pregnant. That wasn't part of the plan at that time, but the twins, Morghan and Krystina, were a rewarding surprise," Charlee said with a smile. "Mateo and I wanted to be as involved as possible in the girls' lives and didn't believe we could do so working twelve- and eighteen-hour days so we opened up a medical practice which specialized in internal medicine. We are today's primary care physicians," she said with a smile. "This type of practice allowed us to spend time with one another and with the girls. We didn't have to be on call every weekend and we didn't have to work evenings," Charlee said.

Charlee paused. "You've been quiet, Doc."

"I'm listening to you," Dr. Montgomery replied calmly.

"Nothing to say yet?" Charlee asked.

"You're very family oriented. You seem to have a good work and home life balance. Do spend time with friends?" the doctor asked.

Charlee's eyes lightened up. "I have two best friends," Charlee said with a smile, "Kellan and Malina. We've been friends since we were eight-years-old. We love to shop, gossip, and eat. We usually do more shopping," Charlee said with a laugh. "We work hard so we treat ourselves big when we go out. We rent town cars and allow ourselves to be chauffeured from store to restaurant to store all day," she said with a giggle.

Charlee was quiet again. "This is about Mateo. I need to get this out before I lose my nerve."

"Ok," Dr. Montgomery replied, "continue."

"Mateo didn't hang out at night. He didn't party with the guys, go to strip clubs, or anything crazy. But Mateo was a golf fanatic. The televisions were always on golf matches and he would travel the world just to play golf. It was extreme. He and his friends would..."

Dr. Montgomery interrupted Charlee. "I'm sorry. Travel the world to play golf? Were you being literal when you said that?"

"Absolutely," Charlee replied.

"Continue," the doctor said.

"He and his friends would take a week or two off at a time, sometimes, and go to golf tournaments all over the world. It used to bother me, but when I realized that he never takes time off from work and he never hangs out, I stopped fussing about it." Charlee shrugged. "I wish I had paid better attention. Thinking back on it... I should have known."

Charlee was quiet for a moment. She looked off for a moment, then caught Dr. Montgomery looking at the clock.

"Do you have any other appointments after me?" Charlee asked.

"I have one appointment in two hours," Dr. Montgomery replied.

"Can you cancel it and I buy the rest of your day?" Charlee asked confidently.

Dr. Montgomery picked up her phone and called her assistant. "Anna, cancel the rest of my day.

"Yes, ma'am," Anna answered.

"I'm all yours," Dr. Montgomery said to Charlee. "What should you have known?"

"What?" Charlee asked.

"Before you asked for my time. You were talking about Mateo and his friends going on golf trips," she reminded.

"Right. I should have known what was going on with Mateo. His friends are fine. Mateo is fine as well, but his friends are pretty," Charlee said.

"Pretty? How so?" Dr. Montgomery said with a smile.

"They were always known as pretty boys. Kyle, Nick, and Fernando were fine as hell. Kyle is a little on the short side, but he was muscular and well defined. His muscles would have given Mr. Universe a run for his money. He had dark, deep set eyes, a low-cut fade, and smooth chocolate skin. Kyle spent too much time in the mirror and he was way too pretty."

Charlee stared off again and took a deep breath before you she continued. "Nick and Fernando are identical twins from the Dominican

Republic. In college they were called double trouble. They used to trick the women into believing one was the other. They slept with anything in a skirt. I used to think they were gay until all of that started. Fernando was the best decorator then and now. I would always consult him when I decided to rearrange furniture or update the house. Nick was the strong silent type. He only talked around people he was comfortable being around. That was the main reason I couldn't figure out why women couldn't tell them apart. They acted completely different."

Charlee shifted in her seat.

"Are you uncomfortable?" Dr. Montgomery asked.

"I'm very uncomfortable. This whole situation is discomforting," she answered.

"Do you want to take a break?" the doctor asked.

"No, I'm fine. Anyway, I loved those guys. Kyle, Nick, and Fernando were like brothers to me. When I knew they were coming over I would cook a big meal and take out the margarita machine. I'd hang out with the guys for a little bit then head out to give them their guy time."

"So, what changed?" Dr. Montgomery asked.

"Well, they always golfed, but when they left town, I could never reach Mateo. I hated it. I used to believe that's when they went to strip clubs and hung out all night at bars. Mateo and I had our worse arguments when he returned from those trips," Charlee said. "What if there is an emergency? I used to ask him," she said and looked at Dr. Montgomery. "He'd shrug and remind me to call 911. He'd ask what could he do if he was out of town. He was right, but that was beside the point. He went on one trip and Morghan broke her arm when she fell wrong during a soccer game. She had to have surgery and she was terrified. All she did was cry for her daddy. I eventually reached him at his room, but he didn't rush back. I feel like as a parent he should have hopped on the first thing smoking and headed home. He only said to me, 'You're a doctor, Charlee, calm her down until I get there.' He didn't return home for two days. She wasn't upset that he didn't come home immediately, but the point is that he put something else in front of his children."

"Does he call you often when you're out with your friends?" Dr. Montgomery asked.

"No, but I call home four or five times a day. He would tell me that I didn't have to call home so much. He told me to just enjoy myself. I just didn't get it." Charlee shrugged. "I asked my friends if they'd experienced anything like that and they told me stories about guys cheating and the wife finding out about it and how the wife went off on him and the side chick in public. It was ridiculous. Anyway, I didn't believe Mateo was cheating while he was out of town, just selfish and inconsiderate. He would come home, we'd argue, have great make-up sex, then all was forgotten." Charlee shrugged again. "I don't know. I figured things would work themselves out, but they didn't. They actually got worse."

"How so?" the doctor asked.

"Mateo and I took turns going out of town. He left more often than I did, but I didn't mind. Anyway, it was my turn. My friends and I planned a girl's trip to Vegas. I was going to use that time to detox from my feelings of insecurity regarding Mateo and to celebrate having an empty nest since the twins were leaving for college soon. Mateo's mother was coming in to town to spend time with the girls before they left for college. She was also low-key baby-sitting for us. They girls were almost eighteen, but we still liked for them to have adult supervision. I was supposed to pick his mother up from the airport, but he had forgotten to leave me her itinerary so I looked it up in his email."

"Does he know you have access to his email?" the doctor asked.

"He does. He gave me the password when they girls were applying for financial aid. They had all of the correspondence sent to him so he could review them, but he never had time so I was doing it," Charlee answered.

"What did you find?" Dr. Montgomery asked.

"What makes you think I found anything?" Charlee asked defensively.

"When you started coming to me, you told me there was 'something' going on with your husband, but you refused to talk about him. Now that you're talking openly about him, I'm assuming everything started with whatever you found in his email," Dr. Montgomery answered.

Charlee rolled her eyes and looked away. "Everything started fifteen years ago, actually," Charlee said with sarcasm and sadness in her voice.

"Tell me about it," the doctor said.

"Let me first say that I never go through my husband's phone, his tablet, or his laptop," Charlee gave her disclaimer.

"I believe you," Dr. Montgomery said.

"So, I opened up his email looking for the itinerary and I couldn't find it. I assumed he deleted it so I went into the deleted messages box. As I scrolled through the deleted messages, I see a subject that read, '15-year Anniversary Celebration'. Mateo was big on celebrations with our college friends and I figured he accidentally deleted the message so I opened it."

Charlee stood up and walked over to the window again. Dr. Montgomery remained silent.

"'See you soon, love.' That's what the message read. I lost my breath. I literally couldn't breathe. My heart started racing and it felt like someone had punched me in my stomach," Charlee said.

Charlee walked back over to the sofa, poured herself a glass of water, and took a sip. Dr. Montgomery waited.

"My husband, Dr. Montgomery, was having an affair for fifteen years. His golfing trip was him celebrating their fifteen-year anniversary."

"Are you going to tell me who she was?" Dr. Montgomery asked.

Charlee shot her a look and busted out laughing.

"SHE!? You want to know who *she* was, Dr. Montgomery?" Charlee asked sarcastically.

Dr. Montgomery remained silent.

"Do you have anything stronger than water?" Charlee asked.

"I don't," Dr. Montgomery answered.

"You ever heard the song called *You, Me, and He* by Mtume?" Charlee asked the doctor.

"I don't think so," Dr. Montgomery answered.

"Well, in the song, a woman and her husband are singing to one another. It starts off with the wife confessing that she has a lover," Charlee shook her head. "She actually said to her husband, 'He's my lover and I'm your wife.'" Charlee chuckled. They go on to sing about how they're living a lie," Charlee looked at the doctor with tears in her eyes. "Mateo and I have been living a lie. Well actually he's the one who has been living a lie."

Dr. Montgomery reached over and slid the box of tissues to Charlee.

"Thank you," Charlee said. "To answer your question, no, I'm not going to tell you who *she* was. But I will tell you who *he* was," Charlee said as she looked at Dr. Montgomery for a response.

Dr. Montgomery said nothing and her face didn't change.

"It was Kyle. Mateo, my husband, the father of my children, my partner in life, my partner in business was a homosexual and had been having an affair with his best friend for the last fifteen years."

"I'm sorry you experienced that, Charlee," Dr. Montgomery said to her.

Charlee wiped her eyes and sipped more water.

"Do you want to continue?" Dr. Montgomery asked.

"Yeah, I'm ok," Charlee answered.

"What happened next?" the doctor asked.

"I started going through all of the emails from Kyle, Nick and Fernando. There were only two from Nick and Fernando confirming their travel dates. There weren't many from Kyle. I guess Mateo permanently deleted them after he read them. Those that were there only mentioned the trips they were attending. There were a few that revealed that he and Mateo were traveling alone, without Nick and Fernando, and there were several where they had exchanged photos of each other. Just when I was ready to stop looking through the computer, I found a hidden folder that was password protected. My poor, stupid, husband... his passwords were always one of the kids' names and our anniversary, but that wasn't it. So, I sat back in the chair for a moment and looked at the anniversary photo of me and Mateo."

Charlee had a sly look on her face when she continued. "So, I tried Mateo and Kyle's anniversary date with Kyle's name and it opened."

Dr. Montgomery's eyebrows were raised.

"Ha! I finally got a reaction out of you, Doc," Charlee said with a psychotic laugh.

"I'm sorry, Charlee," the doctor said.

"No, don't be sorry. I'm glad to see something finally shocked you," Charlee said with a giggle. "Anyway, I almost forgot about his mother. I called her and told her that I wasn't leaving after all. I apologized for the inconvenience and told her that I would send the girls out to see her before they left for college. She was already prepared to get on her plane to come see us so I paid for a car service to gather her bags and take her back home. I called the girls and told them to stay with friends that weekend because I wanted to spend special time alone with their dad. They made a noise letting me know that we were too old to still be fooling around and told me which friends they would be staying with for the weekend. Morghan was certain to remind me that they didn't have any overnight clothing so I sent money to them through CashApp so they could buy a few things from Target to get them through the weekend."

Charlee stopped talking again and looked at her watch.

"You cancelled my appointment and bought out the rest of my afternoon. We have time. What happened next, Charlee?" Dr. Montgomery asked.

Charlee sighed. I found over fifty messages between Kyle and Mateo. I was sick to my stomach. They talked about how much they loved each other and how much they missed each other. The talked about trips to the islands and starting a family of their own when the kids went off to college. I couldn't believe the photos they had exchanged. Kyle and Mateo had taken professional photos wearing matching outfits. They exchanged nude photos and had taken photos of themselves performing sexual acts on one another. After a few hours of printing out photos and emails, I closed the laptop."

"Was there more that you didn't go through?" the doctor asked.

"There sure was, but after everything I saw, I was done. I was disgusted. I was devastated and, in my mind, I was already divorced."

Dr. Montgomery continued to sit in silence.

"Mateo and I shared an office. It was our way of making sure work stayed separate from our family time." Charlee giggled. "Family time. What a joke. Anyway, I took all of the emails and photos and taped them on every wall of our office. I printed out arrows that led him from the front door to our office. He would have thought I had something sweet planned for his return, but would be surprised to see the office. I called my best friends and told them about what I'd found and to tell them that I wasn't going on the trip. They wanted to come over, but I wanted to be alone. I kind of think they wanted to come over just to hurt Kyle and Mateo for what they had done to me. They cried with me, offered to come over again, and again I declined. We hung up the phone and I sat in bed wondering what happened to my life. I got tired of thinking so I took two sleeping pills then went to bed."

"What was on your mind when you went to bed that night?" Dr. Montgomery asked.

Charlee was silent for a few moments. "I wanted to choke him," she answered.

Dr. Montgomery nodded. "How did you feel when you woke up the next day?"

"Unbelievably calm. I thought I dreamt the day before until I heard Mateo enter the house. I heard a second voice and realized that it was Kyle and I could feel my temperature rising. Mateo and Kyle saw the arrows and they followed them to the office. I was sitting on the stairs listening. He entered the office and I heard Kyle gasp. They were both acting hysterically. 'She knows! Mateo, she knows!' he kept saying. 'Calm down!' Mateo said to him. 'She's not here; just give me a minute to figure this out,' he said to him. I eased downstairs and shocked the hell out of them. 'Hello boys,' I said to them. I watched all of the color leave Kyle's face. 'Forgive my manners,' I said to them. 'Happy anniversary,' I said. Neither of them moved. Mateo asked Kyle to leave. Kyle ran his hand down Mateo's back as he walked past him. I wanted to smack the hell out of him. Kyle left and Mateo stood in silence. 'You're not going to say anything?' I asked him. He only asked, 'Where is my mother?' I told him I asked her to reschedule. He remained silent. 'You're really not going to say anything to me, Mateo?' I asked again. He looked around the office and shook his head. He simply said, 'It's finally over,' and he walked out of the office. All I could do was cry."

Dr. Montgomery reached for the box of tissues. She was crying. "I'm sorry, Charlee. Please continue."

"It's fine, Doc. Trust me, it's a situation worth crying over," Charlee said. "Needless to say, I asked him to leave and he left willingly. The twins returned on Sunday morning. They asked when their dad would be returning from his golf trip and I told them he wouldn't be coming back to our house. They were shocked and started asking me fifty-million questions. I simply told them to call him on his cell phone. That was his mess to clean up," Charlee shrugged. "I didn't want any more to do with him or his mess."

"So where do things stand with you and Mateo now?" Dr. Montgomery asked.

"Mateo is completely out of the closet. He and Kyle don't live together probably because the girls are having too hard a time dealing with Mateo's new life. The girls don't want too much to do with him right now. Mateo doesn't want anything to do with me, but he loves his girls so this is hard for him. The girls are of the age where he and I don't have to talk at all. He bought me out of the practice. I'm selling the house when the girls go off to college. And I've been talking to you for months," Charlee giggled, "and finally getting this story out was such a release for me! I can't lie, that song by Mtume used to trigger depression and anger in me, but it came on in my old school playlist last night and I felt nothing. I actually smiled. I've prayed and asked God to help me with the pain and finally, I'm healed!" Charlee said with a smile.

"What's next for you, Charlee?" Dr. Montgomery said with a smile.

"I'm starting a new practice with a couple of ladies from medical school that were looking to step out on faith," she answered.

"And your heart?" the doctor asked.

Charlee smiled. "My heart is ready to receive love when that time comes. This time…just me and he."

Charlee and Dr. Montgomery shared a laugh before Charlee thanked her for her time and left her office.

CHAPTER 7
TIC TOCK BIOLOGICAL CLOCK

It still hasn't sunk in yet. Ohio? What in the world is in Ohio? Five years with this company and they decide to send me to Ohio. I really thought they were kidding. I've lived and worked in Manhattan most of my life. What is a chic, city girl like me going to do in Ohio? What kind of man could I possibly meet in Ohio? A blue-collar bama. No thank you. I'm used to the custom suits, gold cufflinks, Louis Vuitton shoes, and the matching attaché cases. If I'm stepping onto scenes looking as if I belong on the cover of Vogue, I need a man at my side that complements my sophisticated style, not brings it down. I had goals for that special Wall Street brother. We would meet, marry, live in a brownstone on the Upper Eastside, and raise our two children that would attend exclusive private schools. According to my biological clock, I need to be married and pregnant in a year and a half. This move to Ohio is definitely going to set my life goals back. It may sound a bit stereotypical, but I believed most of the men in Ohio would wear powder blue, green, and even yellow suits with matching patent leather dress shoes.

I was trying to be positive so I focused on the benefits of my new job instead of the possible bamas. I loved dressing up for work, but appreciated that I didn't have to wear suits every day. I invested in oxfords, slacks, polos, and khakis. This new style will help me not stand out like a sore thumb, but still highlight my classic city-girl style.

I went to a local club for a business mixer. I wasn't really into partying, but I knew it was time to start looking for male prospects after being here for six months. I stayed after the mixer to see what Ohio nightlife was like. Just as I suspected… bamas. I sipped on my vodka and cranberry and just tried to enjoy the evening until I turned towards the door and saw this fine specimen of a man enter the establishment. This guy was kind of decent. He had smooth, chocolate brown skin and a smile that lit up the dimly lit club. I watched him as he high-fived people in passing. As he walked closer to the bar where I was sitting, I started paying attention to what he was wearing. He was wearing the ugliest mint-green suit with emerald green patent leather shoes.

"I called it," I said to myself.

For a second… and only for a second, I almost forgot about his attire when I realized he was buff. Though the suit was hideous, his arms, shoulders, and chest were snug beneath his clothing. Immediately, the actor Terry Crews popped into my head.

"I wonder if he can flex his chest muscles like Terry," I thought to myself.

I could tell he was big time in this little city and was used to having his way when it came to the ladies. He could have had his way with me that night, but I was blinded by that damned suit! Mr. Ugly Suit was headed in my direction. He was fine, but I wasn't impressed. He eased over to me with that loud suit.

"How you doing pretty lady?" He started. "What's your name?"

"I'm good," I answered. "My name is Nikita Kline."

That was all the information he was getting from me. I hope he didn't think I was easy. No, sir. I'm Nikita Kline, top of the line dime and you have to come correct each and every time.

Ramon was a bama, but he was polite. He insisted on showing me around the town. He believed it was important to know about where you lived and everything it had to offer. Ramon was street savvy and smooth. It was hard to resist his offer so I didn't.

I wasn't comfortable telling him where I lived so I agreed to meet him the following Friday at the same club where we'd first met. I thought this would be an actual date, but Ramon felt like you had to get to know the heart of the city while everything and everyone was still moving so he picked me up at one o'clock in the afternoon.

"Did you know that capital of Ohio was Columbus?" He asked me.

I rolled my eyes. "Yes, I knew that." I wasn't trying to be disrespectful, but that was information I'd learned in the third grade. What I didn't know was the other information he shared. Columbus wasn't the original capital. It has been changed quite a few times. Ohio was rich in culture and the people who lived there took football way too seriously. There was red and gray all over the place. Apparently, those were the school colors of Ohio State University. I knew nothing about football and didn't really care about it, but Ramon showed me the love of the people in that sport. It was corny, but kind of amazing at the same time. What did interest me was the art scene. Columbus was full of art, music, theaters, and museums. I never would have thought that the little town I was staying in was so close to all of this history. There were bars and restaurants in a place call the Short North and a historic town called German Village. I could not believe that this man who was now dressed in bright green pants and a white silk shirt knew this much about history.

Ramon was also very well liked. Everywhere we went he knew someone or someone knew him. He knew the restaurant owners, museum curators, school coaches... I must admit, I was finally impressed. I learned so much about Ohio from him. I thanked him for showing me around town.

"You're welcome. So now can I have your number?" He asked.

I laughed. I completed forgot we never exchanged numbers.

"Sure," I said.

I can't tell if I was more impressed by the date or what may have been hidden beneath those ugly green pants. It had been a year since I had sex so I wasn't sure what was leading my decision.

Ramon wined and dined me for an entire month. When we weren't together, we were on the phone laughing, joking and sharing crazy stories about our lives. When we took our relationship to the next level, he was everything I imagined. He was a slow and intentional lover. Ramon was just what the doctor ordered and I was pleased each and every time. Six more months like this and I figured Ramon would end up a finalist in giving me a child. He continued to wear those ugly suits and matching shoes everywhere we went. It drove me crazy, but I didn't mind after a while because he seemed proud to have an "uptown girl" on his arm. My fears of living in Ohio were calmed; or maybe I was a-dick-ted! Either way, there was finally hope for my love life in Ohio!

Ramon wasn't the Manhattan business man I'd always dreamed of, but he was a true business man in Ohio. He had three phones that rang constantly and it drove me crazy. The traveling made it even worse. Every week, Ramon was in a different state handling business. While I appreciated a hard-working man, I also knew he was messing up my timeline for my biological time clock. We needed to start working on making a baby very soon.

I looked forward to hearing from him daily, but the calls slowed considerably when he was out of town. The calls went from five or six times a day to one or two calls every other day. Suddenly, the calls just stopped. I didn't hear from Ramon for three weeks. I called and called, but he never answered. I sent him text messages and they came and went with no reply.

"What the hell?!" I thought to myself. "Everything was going fine! How did he just disappear?"

Somewhere around week four I got a call from one of his three numbers. I almost didn't recognize it. I felt like a school girl that had just been asked to the prom. I fixed my hair and straightened my shirt, like he could see me, before I answered the phone.

"Hey Ramon," I said like everything was all good.

The female voice caught me off guard.

"Who the hell are you?" She asked.

"Excuse me?" I replied.

"You know what," she started, "I'm sorry. Who is this?"

That's better, I thought to myself. "This is Nikita. Who are you and why are you calling me from Ramon's phone?"

"Dis Ramon's wife, Keesha," she answered.

"Oh shit," I thought to myself.

"I didn't know he was married," I said to her.

"I know," she said. "Ramon does this to every new woman that comes into town. In fact, he has another wife and five kids on the other side of town. Did he take you to Columbus and impress you by talking about history and other bullshit?"

The situation wasn't funny, but I giggled. It was evident that Keesha and I were very different, but similar at the same time.

"Yes, he did."

"Yeah girl, I fell for that BS too. I pay the phone bill so I check it every month. Every time I see a new number that he's calling all the time, I know it's some new chick he done met at that club in Delaware."

I was shocked. She was so calm! This was normal to her, but this was foolishness to me and I didn't want any parts of it or him.

"Ramon hasn't worked in ten years," she continued, "its women all over the place looking for him. I'm surprised I haven't turned him in myself to be honest."

"I know this is none of my business, but why are you still with him?" I asked.

"Girl, I know you slept with him already so you know why I stay!" she said with a hysterical laugh.

This was no longer funny to me at all. Keesha explained that she just wanted me to know who I was dealing with before he started using me to pay for those ugly suits. I thanked her for the information and ended the call.

I felt sick for two weeks; and no, I wasn't pregnant. I just couldn't figure out how I let an ugly suit wearing bama named Ramon play me, Ms. Nikita Kline, top of the line dime. I learned a lot from this mess though. I can't sell myself short for any man. I can be flexible with my standards, but I can't lose myself in the process. I can't allow myself to be impressed by information I can learn on Google.

Signing off... Nikita Kline in Bamatown Ohio.

CHAPTER 8
HO...HO...HO

Business mixers are always the perfect breeding ground for hook-ups, hang-outs, and even full-blown situationships. So when a mixer is held at The Greenbriar Country Club, one of the most beautiful venues on the east coast, any and everything is bound to happen. Let me tell you a little about the Greenbriar. Its ten-thousand square feet of pure elegance and fun. Privacy and pleasure are guaranteed for anyone who walks its beautiful park-like grounds, tees off on its golf course, smokes cigars in the billiard rooms, and sips wine in the sauna. The Greenbriar, in my personal opinion, is the perfect place to get into all types of trouble and that's exactly what happened at this week's mixer.

Every Friday night The Greenbriar was the hang out for the professionals in the area. Doctors, lawyers, judges, accountants, and others looked forward to the weekly business mixer. They networked while relaxing and meeting the newest professionals in the area. Seeing all of those professional men in one place was exciting for me, but I was careful with how much time I spent there. Careful because of men like Ron Valentino.

Ron Valentino was sexy. Actually, everything about him was sexy. He was tall, six-feet, three inches, and Italian. He had thick black hair, piercing gray eyes, and the sharpest goatee I've ever seen. He was thin, but clearly cared a lot about his looks because he would be seen running the track in the park almost daily. He was sharp even when doing that. He always wore matching, designer running suits and new looking sneakers. Ron was the talk of the town. He drove a red, convertible 1968 Oldsmobile Cutlass that looked as if he had it detailed daily. The pipes made it loud, but it was more intriguing than irritating. Ron wanted to be seen whenever he was driving that convertible and believe me, he was always seen. Ron was a surgeon at Jefferson Memorial Hospital and all of the nurses wanted him. I'm comfortable saying the doctors wanted him as well. He was charismatic and carried himself like a king. Ron had it all together, but oh my goodness... he was the biggest ho in the city.

Women would flock to The Greenbriar just to hang out with him and his friends. All of his friends were rich and were attached to the medical profession in some aspect and the women loved it. I went to medical school with Ron and to college with some of the guys that hung out at The Greenbriar so I knew to avoid them.

"Kirsten Kelly!" they would call out to me and laugh, "why you acting like you don't want to hang with us?"

"I'm not acting," I would say and laugh at them as I kept walking.

They always joked on me because I didn't entertain their foolishness. They called me stuck-up, standoffish, all kinds of things. I didn't care though. I not only danced to the beat of my own drum; I created the drum. I was the first Black female in Philadelphia to own a dermatology practice and my practice had taken off within the first year. It's been said that many businesses struggle in the first few years, but I never experienced those challenges. I had a waiting list before the sign was hanging up. So when it came to men, it was a want; not a need. Also, I had standards and those guys were beneath my standards. I'm single and would love to have a nice warm body beside me at night, but I saw the games they played first hand and was not interested in becoming a "Greenie" as they called some of the ladies that frequented The Greenbriar establishment.

My best friend, Rosz Martinez, had planned to come visit just to attend a mixer. Rosz was a Radiologist that specialized in women's health. Rosz was a medical force to be reckoned with. She was double board certified, had her own practice, a team of doctors within her practice, and taught at one of the leading hospitals in Georgia. Rosz was motivated to succeed. She was the first in her family to graduate from college and become a medical doctor. Not only was she brilliant, Rosz was gorgeous. She had smooth almond-colored skin, long, thick and curly jet-black hair, and a smile that lit up any room she entered. She had big brown eyes and a beauty mark that sat just above the end of her right eyebrow. She was thick in the thighs, thin in the waist and had small breasts. Men loved her, but she was selective. In college she dated only two men and both of them were on the fast track of success. The men she dated had to be equally motivated as she was and have a five- and ten-year plan for life because even with all of her accolades, she was always seeking the next big opportunity to grow. You would think that with her beauty, brains, and determination that she would be married by now, but clearly, no one had reached her bar of standards yet. Rosz was my hero... or rather, my she-ro.

"Hey girl!" she yelled into the phone.

"Hey," I yelled back.

"I'll be boarding my plane in about thirty minutes. I'm getting my rental car after the plane lands, then I'm heading to your house."

"Great! I should be out of the hair salon by then. Do you still have the key I gave to you?" I asked.

"Did you really forget that you bought a new house, baller?" she asked with a laugh.

"That was three years ago. Oh my goodness! Has it really been three years since we've seen each other?!" I asked her.

"Yes, it has! We have to stop being so busy, KK," she replied.

"We really do. Well call or text me after you get the car so I can be sure to be home. I'll text you my address in a minute."

"Ok, girl. I'll see you in a few hours. Girl! This mixer is going to be a trip!" she said with excitement.

"Girl, bye!" I answered.

"Yes! I can't wait!"

I laughed and ended the call.

"A trip for you, not for me," I thought to myself.

Rosz arrived and was just as professional as ever. She clearly left work and went straight to the airport. She was still wearing her work clothes. She had on a white, tailored oxford, a black and white striped high-waisted skirt, and red, patent leather high-heeled shoes. She wore silver, chandelier earrings and hair was pulled back into a tight, neat bun.

"Hey, girl!" Rosz screamed as she got out of the car.

"Hey!" I answered.

I ran down to the car and Rosz and I embraced.

"Girl, you look so good!" she said to me.

"So do you! I love that skirt!" I said to her.

I grabbed her bags as she grabbed her pocketbook and make-up kit.

"Your house is beautiful!" she said as she walked in the front door.

"Thank you," I said as I walked towards the stairs. "Come on up. I'll give you a tour when we set your things down."

After the tour, Rosz and I sat down in the den to catch up on old times with a nice bottle of wine.

"I can't believe we've come this far," Rosz said.

"I know right. I remember being in the dorms and we were writing out our five-year plan," I said.

"Yes, now here we are – melanated, educated, and sophisticated!"

We busted out laughing.

"So what time does the mixer start?" she asked.

"It starts at six o'clock, but it starts jumping around seven or eight."

"What are you going to wear?" she asked.

"Dark blue skinny jeans, a white tube top, a coral blazer, and wedge sandals," I answered.

"What? You're not getting extra sexy for tonight?"

"I'm sexy in anything I wear, but no, I'm not getting extra sexy for this crowd."

"Why not?"

"Let me tell you what to expect. It's a ho-fest."

Rosz busted out laughing. "A ho-fest?"

"Sure is. It's literally a meat show for professionals and I'm not interested in being a piece of meat," I said with a straight face.

"Well, I'm here for the fun! I don't expect I'll do anything more than flirt tonight. Tell me about the guys."

"I'm not really concerned with all of the guys, but there is one guy you must be aware of," I said.

Rosz smiled.

"I know that look," I said to her.

"What?" she asked.

"You're looking for a challenge."

"You know me so well. So... tell me about this one challenge, I mean guy."

I shook my head and rolled my eyes as I told her all about the infamous Ron Valentino. We laughed hysterically as we sang the Whodini's song "I'm a Ho."

"I can't believe you call him the 'Italian Stallion'!" she laughed. "He can't be that bad."

"Trust me, he is that bad."

"I won't promise that I'll steer clear of him, KK, but I promise I won't be overthrown by his charming antics," she said with a giggle.

I got dressed then went to the guest room to check on Rosz. I knocked on the door and waited for her to respond.

"Come in," she said from the bathroom.

I entered the guest room and was welcomed by the scent of Rosz's perfume.

"Oh, that smells nice!" I said and started looking through Rosz's beautiful clothing that she had laid out on the bed.

"Thank you," she said as she walked out of the bathroom.

Rosz looked amazing as usual. She had her hair down with her natural curls cascading over her shoulders. She had on natural-looking make-up and bright red lipstick. She wore a tight off-white dress that hugged every curve on her body and nude shoes.

"How do I look?" she asked and turned around so I could see her outfit.

"You look amazing as usual. I'll give you ten minutes before Ron is in your face," I said to her.

Rosz smiled and grabbed her wristlet. "Let's go do some damage," she said and interlocked her arm in mine.

We arrived around seven o'clock and the place was packed. Rosz and I entered and all eyes were glued to the door. Rosz smiled and at least five guys almost knocked down the people in their path to make their way to her. I smiled and walked over to the bar to observe the room and laugh at the guys drooling over Rosz. Ron was holding court with five women, but I know he saw Rosz.

Rosz finally made her way to the bar.

"I can't believe these men are acting like this!" she said as she sipped my drink.

"I told you," I said and ordered another drink for myself.

Rosz wasn't sitting down for five minutes before Ron made his way to the bar.

"Kirsten," he said to me while staring at Rosz, "you didn't introduce me to your beautiful friend."

"Rosz, this is Ron Valentino. Ron, this is Rosz," I said.

"Ron and Rosz," he started. "R&R, just what the doctor ordered," he said with a seductive smile.

Rosz giggled.

I excused myself and walked away humming Whodini's song as I gave Rosz a look.

She giggled again as Ron took a seat beside her. Rosz was officially on her own. I walked around the room and networked with a few of the professionals there. I made my way to the billiard room and was glad to learn that there were some new graduates there looking for employment and mentoring opportunities.

After a few hours I went back to the bar and Rosz and Ron were gone. I called her cell phone and she told me that she and Ron were in the gazebo talking. She told me that she would get a taxi back to my place. I started singing "I'm a Ho" again and Rosz laughed and hung up on me. I sent her a text message and told her I would wait up for her.

I nodded off on the sofa, but was awakened around two o'clock in the morning to Ron's exhaust pipes on his convertible. He and Rosz were leaning against his car and she was giggling. I hated to admit it, but they really looked good together. As I stared at them, I wondered if maybe what Ron needed to calm his ho-ish ways was a good woman at his side.

Rosz came into the house and was floating on cloud nine. She told me about the events of the night and how Ron was nothing like what I described.

"Ok," I said to her.

"Have you ever had a real conversation with him, KK?"

You could tell she was agitated.

"Nope, I'm just very observant. I live here and I watch how he interacts with the women," I answered.

"Well, I think you're wrong," she said almost defensively.

"Well, I hope I am," I answered and walked upstairs to my bedroom.

Rosz stayed for the week. She was a little distant, but I'm sure it was because she could sense my displeasure of her relationship with Ron.

"Listen," I said to her, "I'm sorry for being so judgmental. I was just worried that he would take advantage of you."

"You don't need to apologize. I did jump into this kind of quickly and I'm sure that scared you. I'm sorry. Ron's a nice guy, though."

Rosz spent a few nights with him before returning to Atlanta. I was happy for her. Each time we spoke she and Ron were traveling or planning to travel to a new vacation destination. I'd never known Rosz to not go to work. Maybe this was the break she needed. I still wasn't too sure about Ron, but I trusted Rosz's judgment. Maybe their relationship was going to work after all. Rosz seemed so happy that she had finally found her Mr. Right. I was excited. If anyone could take Ron Valentino, the Italian Stallion, out of ho status it was Rosz.

Thursdays at my practice was pro-bono day. I mostly saw teenagers whose parents couldn't afford to take their children to Dermatologists so all day I heard complaining teens and fussing parents. The day normally ended well after seven o'clock in the evening and was usually exhausted. Thursdays was usually the day I turned off my cell phone until Friday morning, but this day I forgot to turn my phone off. Around seven-thirty in the evening I received a call from Laila. Laila was Rosz's best friend. I figured Laila was calling to ask me to help set up an engagement party for Rosz and Ron. I couldn't believe it had been a year since they'd met already.

"This is some bullsh-," Laila started.

"Laila," I yelled and interrupted. "Calm down!"

"I won't calm down! Ron is a piece of trash! Have you spoken to Rosz? I'm sure you haven't," she answered before I could respond.

Laila proceeded to give me an earful about Ron and his recent behaviors. I was shocked. From what I could gather from her rant, Ron was seeing Rosz and two other women. I wanted to be angry. I even wanted to be sad for Rosz, but all that went through my mind was Whodini's song.

"How did she find out, Laila?"

"She wanted to surprise him so she popped up at his place unannounced and saw a woman leaving his place. The woman looked like his sister so Rosz introduced herself to the woman. The woman introduced herself to Rosz as Yasmeen, Ron's fiancé. Rosz went ballistic. She went on to tell the girl that she was Ron's second."

"Have mercy," I said as I sat in my car. "Wait... second? What do you mean his second?"

"She told the girl, Yasmeen, that Ron was caught with one of the nurses at his friend's office and how he begged Rosz to come back. Yasmeen asked Rosz how long they were involved and Rosz told her about a year. Yasmeen learned that Rosz lived out of town, but Ron had been telling her he was in Atlanta on business."

"How is she doing?" I asked.

"Rosz is in bad shape, Kirsten. She's hurt and disappointed. She saw a bunch of red flags: lying, not being where he said he would be, cancelling dates, not showing up for vacations, but she never confronted him. She was always just so glad to see him that she just let things pass."

"I wonder why she never called and told me any of this," I said.

"She was embarrassed. She jumped in quickly and was always bragging about Mr. Right. I'm sure she didn't want to hear the 'I told you so' from you."

I felt kind of bad, but then I couldn't help but remember that hos don't change. "I was hoping that meeting Rosz would have changed him because she's such an amazing person. Men like him will never be satisfied with one woman – no matter how great she is. Ron is a ho. Point blank, period."

I called Rosz the next day, but she didn't answer. She finally picked up after a week.

"Hey girl," I said to her.

"Hey."

"I spoke to Laila," I said.

Rosz was quiet.

"Are you ok?" Rosz asked.

"I will be."

"Rosz..."

"I don't need or want your 'I told you so', KK."

"I wasn't going to say that, Rosz. I just wanted to check on you," Kirsten said.

"I don't want you to start singing Mary J. Blige's song either."

"Huh?" Kirsten said,

"Don't start singing Mary's song, Mr. Wrong!" Rosz emphasized.

Kirsten laughed. She was glad her friend still had her sense of humor in the midst of a broken heart.

"Well, I learned my lesson, KK."

Kirsten was silent.

"My Mr. Right was actually Mr. Wrong. You told me, KK. You told me that he was a ho and I thought I could change him. He showed me who he was with the nurse and I didn't believe it. Yeah, I learned my lesson, KK. When someone shows you who they are the very first time, believe them."

CHAPTER 9
OUT TO SEA

I'm a military brat. You know, one of those people who had a parent in the military that had them traveling all over the world because of their military responsibilities. Drove me crazy. I told myself I would never date a military man. They were gone for unpredictable amounts of time, never wanted to settle down, and when they did they were prone to lie and cheat. Forgive me, I could be a little biased. That was my life, or rather, my parents' lives. In any case, it was not going to be my life. Period.

I enjoyed partying and did it often. Me and the girls used to spend a lot of time traveling and in the clubs. We met all types of guys, but usually ended up in one-nighters – nothing serious. Now don't go judging me; I'm not a loose woman, I just don't like to be tied down to anything or anyone. Probably a result of being a military brat. Whatever problem you think I may have, let me help you – it's my parents' fault.

Anyway, I have a story for you. It might actually surprise you. Buckle up... this is a bumpy ride.

My friends and I were partying at Club Royal Blue in Norfolk, Virginia when I met Dante' Strong. Doesn't his name sound sexy? Dante' Strong. Looking back on it, sounds more like trouble. I was sitting at the bar resting my feet. I had on four-inch stilettos and they were hot! Set my outfit off nicely, but lawd did they hurt if I stood up too long. So, anyway, I'm sitting at the bar and this dude walks up and got way too close to me.

"What's up beautiful?" he asked.

I saw the dog tag hanging under his t-shirt. "Hello," I answered.

"Can I buy you a drink?" he asked.

"Sure," I said with a smile and he called the bartender over.

The bartender motioned at us.

"What you drinking?" he asked

"Double Hennie on the rocks," I said confidently.

The sailor smiled at me and addressed the bartender, "Give me the same," he said.

"What's your name?" he asked.

"Nay-Nay," I said.

He smiled again. "You're not going to tell me your real name?" he asked.

"LaNay," I told him.

I know what you're thinking; I said I didn't want a military man, but here I am entertaining this dude. Well, if he's going to spend money on Hennessey for the rest of the night, I'll listen to whatever the hell he wants to talk about. He seemed like he had his head on straight and after a couple of rounds of Hennie, he even looked half-way decent.

We talked... well, he did most of the talking, I was drinking. He was a gentleman, though. He walked me to my car and I gave him my number even though I wasn't feeling the fact that he was in the Navy. He called me and came by my apartment a few times. He always called me at the weirdest hours and he would always block the number.

"Why won't you give me your number, Dante'?" I would ask.

"I'm never in one place, baby. I'm almost always TDY, it's just easier for me to call you," he would say.

That's exactly why I hated military men. TDY, or temporary duty assignment, was the reason military men were always away doing something. If they weren't deployed to some unknown, undisclosed place then they were on some assignment slinging their man meat and breaking hearts.

"And you don't have a cell phone?" I would ask.

"I always lose them, baby. Come on now, don't ruin this moment," he would say.

I was the queen of throwing shade so I did... for a whole week. He finally gave me a telephone number to the barracks and I felt pretty good about that. I was back on top of things. Large and in charge. If I was going to play this game with him, I was going to be the one holding all of the cards.

Dante' and I were together for six months. I know, I know... I gave in! What can I say?! His man meat got me hooked! No, for real though, I liked everything about him. He was attentive, he was a nice dresser, he liked Hennie, and he liked spending time with me – when he wasn't on some undisclosed assignment. It was frustrating at times, but it was nice more often.

I knew the time was coming, but didn't realize that it would come so soon. Dante' was deploying. He was going out to sea for a year. According to him it could have been longer. I knew it was coming, but I was sad. I couldn't believe I was actually sad! I found myself thinking about him and wanting to spend all of my time with him.

Dante' finally left. He wouldn't let me take him to the port because he said it would make him sad. Liar. I was actually going to wait for that bastard.

Anyway, long story short, after waiting for four months I decided to embark upon some retail therapy to get Dante' out of my head for a while. I drove over to the mall in Hampton. I walked into Victoria Secret to get something cute and sexy for Dante's return. Spent almost two-hundred dollars on lingerie and body scents when I walked out and ran smack dead into Mr. Out to Sea, Dante' Strong.

Dante' looked as if he'd seen a ghost. I looked at him holding the hand of some woman with three children in tow. There was a ring on his left hand. All I could do was shake my head.

"Hello, Dante'," I said to him, "welcome home," and I walked past them.

I never spoke to him again after that.

From the very beginning I knew not to date military men. I learned two things from Mr. Strong: When a man shows you who he is, believe him. Also, always go with your gut.

Signed... Nay Nay from VA.

The Officer Was Not a Gentleman!

CHAPTER 10
BROKE, BUSTED AND CAN'T BE TRUSTED

I can't remember a time when I wasn't fascinated by cars. I loved the smell of the interior, the crispness of the leather in high-end cars, the sleek design of sports cars, the strength of pick-up trucks, the ruggedness of off-road vehicles... I could go on for days. By the age of five, I owned more than three hundred Hot Wheels vehicles.

I was the family freak by the age of ten. Not only could I identify almost every vehicle – car or truck – on the road, I could tell the vehicle by the revving of its motor. My mother was amazed and annoyed at the same. She could never figure out where this fascination came from. My dad was tragically killed in a car accident. My family believed my addiction came as a result of the accident, but he died when I was five-years old so there goes that theory.

I wanted to be a mechanic, but my mother wanted me to get a job where I made a lot of money.

"Tally," she would say, "you need a career that can pay bills and put food on the table. If you want to fix cars on the side, that's fine, but you're going to get an education!"

I heard that speech whenever I mentioned cars and school in the same sentence. I used to mouth the words as she said it. A few times she caught me so I had to be sure to look remorseful. Some Trinidadian mothers, like my own, were good for throwing a slipper at your head if they thought their children were sassing them.

My mom, Karen, made sure I not only attended college, but I had to graduate with honors. Growing up in Alexandria and knowing I could find a job at any auto shop in my hometown, I decided on Howard University.

I graduated and quickly found a job at an up and coming company called Avex. Avex specialized in shipping high-end cars and parts for their exclusive distributors. It was a good job, but I wanted to be close to cars. I was great at Avex, but needed to smell the oil and leather of the cars. I knew cars, but didn't have any formal training.

I was given an opportunity to sell vehicles at Kashouty Volkswagen. The manager took a chance on me because of my love for cars. Avex paid my bills and Kashouty fueled my passion for cars. While working at Kashouty, I was approached by a man pretending to purchase an Audi A8. Audis were hard to sell for some, but a piece of cake for me. By the end of the demonstration, the customer offered me a job. It turns out he was a sales manager at another dealership and had heard about my sales skills. He wanted to experience them for himself.

"How long have you been selling vehicles young lady?" he asked me.

"About a year," I answered.

"You make good money?" he asked.

"That's kind of personal," I said with a smile.

"Well, do you?" he asked more directly.

"I do," I answered, "but I don't do this for the money. I do it for my love of vehicles."

The gentleman handed Tally his card.

"When you really want to get paid to do what you love, call me," he said. He put on his sun glasses and left the dealership.

Tally stared at the card and was undecided for just a moment. She called him the very next day.

Tally started at Rosenthal Jaguar three weeks later. She loved the transition from Kashouty to Rosenthal. The atmosphere was different, the clientele was exclusive, and her paychecks were much larger. Between satisfying her mother by working with Avex and her passion for cars at Rosenthal, Tally had the best of both worlds.

Tally met Marquis Morrison almost immediately after starting at Rosenthal. It was evident Marquis was a collector and he preferred the Mercedes Benz. He would buy and trade frequently and continued this process every year when there was a significant change to the model or if he simply wanted an upgrade for the new year. Marquis kept Tally's pockets lined.

"I want a silver one this year," Cassandra said.

"Whatever you want," he would usually reply.

"That is one lucky woman," Tally thought to herself. Not only was he driving a nice whip every year or two, she got one as well.

Tally remembered Marquis telling her that he worked in real estate, but she wasn't sure of what he did exactly. She only knew he was rolling in the dough!

Marquis right on time this year. The new S-Class had premiered. So far, Tally had sold six and it was only the sixth of the month. These babies pretty much sold themselves, but Tally's vehicle knowledge closed the deals. People, especially men, loved it when a woman knew her stuff under the hood of a car and loved it even more when it was done in a pencil skirt.

"Welcome back, Mr. Morrison," Tally said to him.

"Tally, we've been associates for years. Please call me Marquis."

I couldn't help but laugh. We had this conversation every time he came in.

It was evident that Marquis was attracted to Tally, but she knew two very distinct things about him. Number one, he had a woman – Cassandra. Number two, Marquis looked like a dark brown iguana. He was unattractive, but those commission checks made it tolerable.

"Tally," Marquis called out.

"Yes sir, Mr..."

He shot Tally a look.

"Marquis," she said and smiled.

"Is everything in order? Are we done?" he asked.

"We are," I said and handed him his keys and complimentary key chains.

"Great. Come, have lunch with me," he said. If he didn't look like an iguana it may have come across seductively.

We were encouraged to have lunch with clients for marketing purposes so I agreed.

"Where should we meet?" I asked him.

"Fyve," he answered. "Do you know where it is?" he asked.

"It's at The Ritz-Carlton in Pentagon City. Yes, I'm familiar with it," I answered.

"Great. I'll see you at six o'clock."

"That's more like dinner," I said cautiously.

"A meal is a meal," he said with a smile as he was escorted to his vehicle.

The meal was exquisite as usual. The conversation was even better. I know you shouldn't judge a book by its cover and it's evident you should judge a lizard by his scales. Marquis looked better and better during our meal. He was very charismatic, he knew how to hold intelligent conversation, and he loved cars. It was amazing how much he knew. I had never met anyone who loved cars as much as I did.

"So how does your husband feel about you selling cars to all of these handsome men?" he asked.

"I'm not married," I said with a laugh.

"So, who takes care of you?" he asked seriously.

"I take care of me," I answered jokingly.

"Oh, excuse me! I thought for sure you were off the market. I would have asked you out long ago!"

"This is supposed to be a business dinner," I started, "I think you're flirting with me," I said.

"We are talking business," he joked. "Tell me how you got into selling cars."

"Well, I've loved cars my entire life..." I started. I went on to tell him about Howard and my job at Avex. He was very impressed.

"Your turn," I said.

Marquis sipped his wine. "What do you want to know?" he asked.

"Cassandra," I said matter of fact.

Marquis laughed. "What about her?"

"How long have you two been married?"

"Married?!" he said with a laugh. "I would never have put a ring on her finger."

"Wow. Why not? You buy cars, clothes, and jewels for her. Why not marriage?"

"Woman, you spend all of your time at the dealer selling and test-driving cars. You don't see what goes on in the business office."

I felt a little foolish because he was right.

"We bought vehicles, but she paid for her own car and I paid for my own."

I smiled.

"Now that we're past that, when is our next date?" he asked seriously.

Tally laughed.

She and Marquis became exclusive almost immediately after their second date.

Marquis traveled often, but when he was in town, he spent all of his free time with Tally. Between his charm, his love for cars, the money he was spending, his flair for fashion, and his insatiable sex-drive, Tally was able to see past the iguana. After an abnormally nurturing night of intimacy, Tally asked Marquis to move in with her.

"Are you sure about that?" he asked without flinching.

"Absolutely," she answered as she ran her fingers across his chest.

"Will you allow me to take care of you?" he asked.

"You take care of me now," she started. "You make me smile. We share secrets, meals, ourselves," she said with a smile. "You definitely take care of me already."

"I mean financially. Are you ok with me depositing money into your account to help with bills and things?" he asked seriously.

Tally was screaming inside, but calmly answered, "I'm ok with that."

Tally had forgotten about Marquis' request, but he didn't.

"Hey, did you take care of that banking situation?"

"Not yet," she answered. "I'll go down there first thing in the morning. Oh, and before I forget..." Tally started.

"The new Maybach is out," Marquis finished her sentence with a smile. "Let me know when you get to work. I'm only buying from you."

Tally smiled. She knew that commission check was going to be a nice edition to her savings account. Tally test drove cars all day at the dealership. She couldn't wait to drive the Maybach through town to flaunt. It wasn't hers, but it would be close enough to it when she drove it while he was in town.

Tally went down to the bank and added Marquis as an authorized user on her savings and checking accounts. He had full access to make deposits and withdrawals. He made that recommendation in case she lost her bank card or in the event of an emergency and Tally agreed without reservation.

Tally was in love. She couldn't believe she was in love after only eight months. When Marquis was in town, he and Tally spent time at car shows, at the race track admiring the "pit", and discussing Tally's future plan to own an auto-body shop. She knew so much about cars and trucks Marquis convinced her to save every check from Avex to put towards the business.

Tally continued working at Avex and Rosenthal. She worked harder than ever to save so she could open the shop with Marquis as her business partner.

Marquis went away on business. It didn't matter how much Marquis called or how often he deposited money into her account, Tally missed him. She appreciated the text messages and video calls, but she wanted him at her side more often.

Marquis had been gone for almost two weeks which was unusual, but Tally trusted him and he continued to call regularly.

"When are you coming back?" she asked him sadly.

"I'll be home in your arms soon, love," he replied.

The doorbell rang.

"Are you expecting company?" Marquis asked.

"No," she said standing up to go to the door.

"Its probably a delivery service. I'll call you back in a few," she said.

"Ok, dear," he answered.

Tally opened the door and was met by two uniformed men. There was no mistaking the uniforms of these men – they were police officers.

"Good evening, ma'am. Is Charles Moore at home?" he asked.

"I'm sorry, you have the wrong address," Tally said.

"I was told that he lives here. It's not too many Maybachs in the area and the car is usually parked in the driveway here," he said as he motioned to the side of the townhouse.

"Marquis Morrison lives here and drives the Maybach. That's my boyfriend. What's going on?" Tally asked seriously.

"Ma'am do you mind of we come in to speak privately?" the officer asked.

"Not at all, come in," Tally said and stepped to the side to let them in.

Officers Coleman and Bennett entered the home and sat when invited.

They explained that Charles Moore, also known as Marquis Morrison is a thief.

"Do you have a picture of him?" Tally asked.

"I do," Officer Coleman replied.

He pulled out a photo labeled 'Charles Moore' and Tally's eyes widened.

"That's Marquis," she said slowly and sadly. "We've been together for almost a year," Tally continued.

"Where is he now?" Officer Coleman asked.

"He's out of town on business," she answered.

"What does he do?" Officer Bennett asked.

In that moment Tally realized that she didn't know what he did or what company he worked for.

"I don't know," she answered. "I only know he works in real estate."

"Where did he live before he moved in?" Officer Bennett asked.

Tally realized that he'd always taken her out for meals and ended up back at her placed. He moved in so quickly she never thought about where he lived.

Tally's eyes watered up and she looked at Officer Coleman.

"You said he was a thief. There's nothing missing from my home," she said as she looked around noticing nothing was missing.

"Money ma'am. Is he on any of your bank accounts?" Officer

Bennett asked.

Tally grabbed her phone and opened up her banking app. Her eyes widened again.

"It's gone," she whispered. "It's all gone!" she screamed and threw her phone onto the sofa.

Tally told the officers about the business account and the household accounts where Marquis had access. She showed them her accounts which noted a zero balance. The checking account had more than eight thousand dollars in it when she checked it last night. The business account had more than twenty thousand dollars. Tally was devastated.

The officers told Tally of his twenty-two aliases and the millions he had stolen from other women.

"I don't want to hear anymore!" she shouted. "How do we stop this thieving bastard?" she asked.

"Does he suspect you know anything?" Officer Coleman asked.

"No. We were on the phone when you rang my bell," she answered angrily.

"When you do you expect him to return?"

"Any day now," she answered.

"As soon as he's here, keep him here. Don't compromise your safety, but call us immediately."

"The only person's safety you need to worry about is his," she said.

Officer Coleman gave Tally his card and the officers left her house.

Tally paced the room trying to decide her next move. She wanted to report the incident to the bank immediately, but didn't want to alert Marquis or Charles or whatever his name was.

Tally calmed herself and called Marquis back.

"Hello love," he answered.

"Hey..." Tally answered and continued as if nothing happened.

The following day, Tally came home from work and smelled stewed chicken brewing. She was instantly angered.

"That bastard is back," she said to herself.

Marquis peaked from the kitchen then walked toward Tally.

"Hey! I thought I heard the door!" he said and embraced her.

Tally had a harder time pretending than she thought she would have.

He was looking like a lizard once again. A lying lizard.

"Hey love," she said.

"What's the matter?" he asked.

"Long day," she answered.

"Well I've started dinner. You go up, shower, and come back down for dinner," he said.

"I have a better idea," Tally started. "You go shower, dry off, and climb into bed. I'll shower in the guest room. I have a surprise for you," she said with a devilish grin.

Tally waited until she heard Marquis singing in the shower before she called Officer Coleman.

"Officer Coleman," he answered.

"This is Tally McCoy," she whispered. "Marquis, I mean Charles is here!"

"On my way," Officer Coleman said and ended the call.

"I'm ready, love," Marquis called out from the bedroom.

Tally had adorned herself in latex, leather, and chains and entered the bedroom.

Marquis was shocked. "Never saw this side of you, but I like it!"

Tally smiled as she handcuffed Marquis to the bedpost.

"Handcuffs?! Wow!" Marquis said. "What's next?!" he said excitedly.

"Bars," Tally said calmly.

"Bars?" Marquis asked confused.

The doorbell rang.

"Yep, bars, for probably ten to twenty years," Tally said as she wrapped herself in her bathrobe to open the front door.

"Tally! Come back here! Where are you going?!"

Officers Coleman, Bennett, and two plain clothes officers followed Tally to her bedroom where Marquis was struggling to break loose from the handcuffs.

The officers laughed, released him, and read him his Miranda rights as they cuffed him.

"At least get my shorts!" Marquis yelled out.

Tally gave the officer a pair of shoes, a t-shirt, and pants. The officers helped Marquis get dressed then left the house.

Tally called the bank and filed the appropriate claims.

"I'm sorry this happened to you, Ms. McCoy. The investigation takes thirty to forty-five business days if you provide us with a copy of the police report. I expect there won't be any problems with the insurance company covering the stolen funds.

Tally ended the call then poured herself a drink. She walked around the bedroom and found Marquis' cell phone on the nightstand. She opened the phone and scrolled through the recently called numbers.

"Cassandra," she read. Tally sipped her drink and hit the send button.

"Hey baby," Cassandra answered.

Tally was silent for a moment. "Cassandra, this is Tally."

"Tally? Who are you and why do you have my husband's phone?" Cassandra asked.

Tally chuckled. "None of that matters. All that matters is that your husband is a liar, a cheat, and a thief, and he never told me he was married. He stole all of my money and I expect he's been stealing yours as well. You need to check all of your accounts to be sure he didn't do to you what he did to me. You can call Officer Coleman at the county jail for information about his arrest," and with that Tally ended the call.

Tally finished her drink and called her mother. She told her everything that took place from start to finish and in typical Karen McCoy fashion she reminded her daughter of the importance of paying attention to the big things.

"Had you been focused on your future at Avex and not those cars, you wouldn't have been in this situation!"

Tally couldn't help but laugh out loud. "I've learned my lesson mom."

"Really?" she started. "What did you learn?"

"Looks can be deceiving. Sometimes rich acting men are really broke, busted, and they can't be trusted."

CHAPTER 11
THREE THE HARD WAY

Dr. Monroe was cleaning off the table in his office when a visibly disturbed parent entered.

"Hey Doc," Candice said as she knocked on his office door.

"Hey Candice, what's up?" he said cheerfully.

"I know I don't have an appointment," she started, "but my daughters are out of control and I'm at my wits end. I... I just don't know what to do anymore," she said as she sighed.

"It's fine, Candice, have a seat," he said as he motioned to a chair.

The troubled mother took a seat in a chair in front of Dr. Monroe's desk and he sat at a table across from her.

"Being a single parent to twin girls must be a challenge, but we're here to help you, Candice. Tell me about what's going on."

"Both of my daughters were good when they were little girls; you know, when they were small, filled with giggles, and innocent," she said with a weak smile.

Dr. Monroe smiled.

"They were pleasant, friendly, and sweet... then all of a sudden they hit puberty, and everything changed. I mean, I know girls go through things, but I was a child and I never did half the things they're doing!" Candice finished.

"Try to calm down, Candice. What types of things are they doing?"

Candice was quiet for a moment then she looked around the room. Sensing she needed privacy, Dr. Monroe got up and shut the door.

"You can be open and honest here, Candice. Tell me, what types of things are they doing?" he repeated.

"Both of them are sneaking out the house, both are promiscuous. One was caught kissing a girl in school and I even heard a rumor about the other one having a three-some. I just feel like they're on the road to destruction, Doc. I feel like I've lost them," she said sadly.

Dr. Monroe stood up and walked behind his desk. He looked at the pictures of his beautiful family, sighed, then sat down behind his desk.

"Candice, I want to tell you a story. Do you have time?"

Candice shrugged. "Sure. The girls are in the movie room," she said as she motioned to one of the rooms in the facility.

"Mr. and Mrs. Carter Hudson welcomed three beautiful girls on February 14, 1980," he started.

"Oh my goodness," Candice interrupted, "they had triplets!?"

Dr. Monroe laughed. "Indeed, they did. Identical triplets. Their names were Kalila, Vida, and Amanda. The Hudson's had some challenges with conceiving so when they were finally able to get pregnant and delivered three healthy baby girls, they wanted them to always remember that they were loved from the very beginning so all of their names were derivations of love."

"What do you mean?" Candice asked.

"Kalila was an Arabic name which meant 'dearly loved'. Vida's name was a short form of Davida, which was Hebrew and it meant 'beloved.' Amanda's name had a Latin root which meant 'she is loved.'"

"Oh wow," Candice said, "that was really creative. Kalila, Vida, and Amanda. And those names are beautiful," she said with a smile.

"They were truly loved and being born on Valentine's Day was only a plus for the family. Kalila arrived ten minutes before Vida and Vida arrived two minutes before Amanda so everyone always considered Kalila to be the oldest. Anyway, their parents were very hard workers and they were very successful. They owned one of the largest outdoor sporting goods stores in Virginia called Neo Wavez. Their store was incredible. They sold everything from backpacks to motorboats. The store was a one-stop-shop for the adventurer. During their youth, their parents kept them busy by having them work at the store in hopes that it would keep them away from boys and out of trouble, but it did just the opposite. They had great personalities and were very popular. Their father was stressed out from all of the attention the girls received while working in the store," he said with a chuckle. "Aside from being triplets, they were beautiful and friendly," Dr. Monroe laughed. "So while the world came to know them as the 'Triple Threat' their father always referred to them as his 'Triple Heart Attacks.'"

Candice laughed. "Why were they known as the triple threat?" she asked.

"They were gorgeous," he said as he stared out of the window.

"They each had an exotic look about them," he said.

"I thought they were identical," Candice said. "I mean, you said they were triplets, but how could each of them have their own look?"

Dr. Monroe chuckled. "I don't know how to explain it, exactly. They were identical, but different. They were tall and had cocoa brown skin. Kalila had hazel eyes and a mole that sat just in front of her right ear. Vida and Amanda had grey eyes. Both of them had moles as well, but I don't remember where they were. Maybe that was the difference," he shrugged. "They had long, dark brown hair, almond shaped eyes, and beautiful white teeth that glistened when they smiled." He chuckled again. "Thinking back on it, they each had braces at the exact same time. But everything changed when the girls went to high school. Mr. Hudson had to prepare himself to loosen up the reigns on his girls because they became active in sports and other extracurricular activities. They hid their lifestyles pretty well," he said as he nodded his head, "but everything kind of came out at some point."

"Wow," Candice said.

"Wow is right. It's kind of a lot, but I'm going to start from the beginning and I'll start with Vida," he said.

Candice leaned back in her seat and got comfortable. She was determined to learn how this story would help her with her girls.

"Aside from beauty, Vida was a genius," he said. "She graduated from high school at the top of her class and went on to Cornell University where she double-majored in Foreign Languages and Political Science and Government. Never in my life had I met anyone that spoke seven languages. Vida could hear a language and learn it fluently within two months. It was an unbelievable gift," he said with widened eyes. "She went on to become a translator for the United States government. Vida was often flown all around the country with top government officials to translate conversations as well as documents. People envied Vida's life," he said. "She made good money, she was free to come and go as she pleased, she lived in a beautiful home in a prestigious neighborhood. Vida was living the life. Little did people know, though, Vida was miserable."

"Miserable? Her life seemed great for a young single woman," Candice said.

"Exactly!" Dr. Monroe said. "But she wasn't a single woman! She was married to a man named Marcus. Vida met Marcus while on assignment in Russia. Marcus was the personal assistant to a government official and he and Vida met during a conference. It was a whirlwind romance for those two weeks and they agreed to meetup when they returned to the United States."

"Awww... that was beautiful," Candice said.

Dr. Monroe looked at her squarely in the eye. "Not really," he said seriously. "Vida had been trying to get pregnant for over two years with no luck. Meanwhile, she had to put up with Marcus' disrespectful children and their equally disrespectful mother. Vida, as beautiful and successful and intelligent as she was, became very insecure very quickly. Not only did her husband seem detached from her, the one thing she thought would capture his heart, a child, she couldn't provide. Vida began to feel less than a woman because she wasn't able to give her husband any children. All she dreamed of was having twins or triplets, like her parents, for this handsome man."

"Wow," Candice interrupted.

"Wow is right. Could you imagine living a pretend life?" he asked Candice seriously.

She didn't answer.

"Neither could I. Marcus' children spent every other weekend with Vida and her husband, and she had to pretend she was happy to see those bad ass children each and every time. It was torturous for her."

"What made them so terrible, Doc? Like, you said they were disrespectful, but what types of things did they do?" Candice asked seriously.

"They would enter the house and never part their lips to speak to

Vida. They would speak to their dad and walk past her like she was just another trinket in the house. She was invisible to them, but that's probably because she was invisible to him. She would tell them to do something like wash the dishes or take out the trash and they wouldn't move. They didn't even look at her. Once Marcus came home from work and asked Vida where the children were and she told him they were in their bedrooms, but they weren't. They were in the park but Vida didn't know because they left the house and never told her. You would think that Marcus would have went off about that and he did," Dr. Monroe said.

"Good!" Candice said and clapped her hands in approval.

Dr. Monroe smiled. "Nope, Marcus went off on Vida for not paying close enough attention to his children."

Candice shook her head.

"Marcus never corrected their behavior and when Vida would address him about the things they did or did not do it would lead to big fights. He would say cruel things to her like, 'You don't have any children so you wouldn't understand,' or 'You don't have the mommy gene so none of this would make sense to you.' Vida would cry, sometimes unconsolably, to her sisters. They told her to leave him, but she stayed. To add to the drama and disrespect, Lucretia, the kids' mother, would call him at inappropriate times of the morning and night."

"What was she calling about?" Candice asked.

"Everything and nothing. She was receiving seventeen hundred dollars a month in child support, but always needed more for this bill or that bill. She lived outside of her means and expected Marcus to pay for it. Her requests angered Vida and whenever she spoke to Marcus about Lucretia, he became irate and was quick to remind her that *his* kids were none of *her* business. He always found a way to remind her that she didn't have any children. Often he would tell her that when it came to her becoming pregnant that she was the problem."

"No!" Candice said.

"Yes. What he actually told her was that he knew she was the problem. He would motion to his children and say, 'We both know there's nothing wrong with me because I don't shoot blanks.' Vida became depressed and nothing could pull her out of it. She ended up seeing a fertility specialist, but she was forced to go alone because Marcus refused to go with her."

"Why didn't she take her sisters?" Candice asked.

"She didn't discuss it with her sisters at the time because she didn't want to hear any of their negative feedback. Kalila was good for the 'Didn't I tell you...' speech and Amanda was notorious for her 'You should have listened to Kalila when she said...' speech," he said.

"Why didn't she take her mother?" Candice asked.

"She didn't know what was going on with Vida and Marcus. Vida never wanted to tell her mother because, in her eyes, her parents' marriage was picture perfect. She didn't want them to know she was experiencing such challenges in her own marriage."

Candice dropped her head in sadness for Vida.

Dr. Monroe smiled. "There's more to the story, Candice."

Candice nodded her head and took a deep breath.

"At the suggestion of her therapist and fertility specialist, Vida began going to the gym a few times a week to relieve some of the stress in her life. One day while at the gym, Vida was approached by a guy named DJ that frequented the establishment."

"What's a beautiful woman like you doing here by yourself?" he asked her.

"People go to the gym by themselves all the time," she answered.

"It's different with you, though. You're always here by yourself – day in and day out – alone."

Vida ignored him.

"What is your husband smoking?" DJ asked seriously.

"He has a demanding job and I'm working from home now I just want to put my free time to good use," she said.

"DJ noticed that she was using the pull-down machine incorrectly so he offered his assistance. Vida was lonely and desperate for attention and affection. The fact that DJ was very attractive and smelled like heaven didn't help," he chuckled. "Vida was ashamed being married and thinking about another man. She and Marcus hadn't been together sexually in more than a month and she was weak."

"Why hadn't they been together?" Candice asked.

"Because he was mean and nasty to her," Dr. Monroe said. "She was punishing him by withholding sex."

"Wow," Candice said. "Finish, Doc! This is getting good!" Candice said seriously.

Dr. Monroe chuckled. "Well, Vida couldn't wait to get back to the gym to see DJ. She went out and purchased some cute workout gear with matching shoes. She did all kinds of things, subtly of course, to be noticed by DJ."

"She was flirting with danger," Candice said with wide eyes.

"Yes, she was," Dr. Monroe said. "Vida approached DJ the next time she saw him and invited him out for coffee."

"So what's on your mind?" DJ asked Vida.

"I'm unhappy in my marriage. My husband is an ass, so I haven't been giving this ass to him, but I really want to give it to you," she said to him with a sly smile.

"Wow!" Candice yelled.

Dr. Monroe chuckled.

"Finish, Doc, finish!"

"DJ was stunned. 'Are you sure this is what you want?' he asked her.

"I don't want anything serious, but I do want you," she said to him.

"Vida and DJ ended up at his house. His place was amazing and he was the perfect gentleman. He offered her wine and strawberries, not realizing that she didn't need to be wined or dined. She just wanted to know what affection felt like again. DJ asked Vida how she wanted it and she told him that she wanted to be fucked and he happily obliged."

Candice listened to Dr. Monroe in wide-eyed wonder. "Wow," she whispered.

"Wow is right," he said. "You haven't heard the half of it. Vida was so into it she didn't realize that DJ never put on a condom. Just as quickly as she realized it, she stopped thinking about it let herself enjoy the moment with him. She allowed DJ to finish, she cleaned up and she headed home. Vida drove home on cloud nine. She almost ran a red-light imagining DJ inside of her. She arrived home and Marcus hadn't gotten home yet. She showered and started to prepare dinner when Marcus came into the house with roses and wine."

"Hey beauty," he said to her. "She smiled as she looked at the flowers. It was obvious to her that Marcus wanted to kiss and make up, but all Vida could think about was DJ's hard penis throbbing inside of her. She tried to tell him that she was tired, but it had been a long time for him and he wasn't taking no for an answer. Vida let Marcus bend her over the kitchen table and she remained motionless while he stroked her from behind. Vida went to bed that night thinking of DJ and hoping to see him soon."

Dr. Monroe got up from the desk to get some water from his refrigerator. He offered Candice a bottle, but she declined.

"Doc, I just want you to finish this story!" she yelled.

Dr. Monroe laughed out loud. "Ok, Candice. So, their affair continued. Vida and DJ fell in love and she started pulling away from Marcus. He could sense that something was different. She wasn't saying anything about having children or the fertility clinic. Vida was content with the fact that she would never have Marcus' children and she was finally ok with that. She wasn't complaining about his disrespectful children or Lucretia. Marcus noticed something in Vida he hasn't seen in years. Vida was unbothered and undisturbed. Vida was at peace and he wanted to be a part of that. Sometime later Vida received a reminder text from the fertility clinic. She wasn't overly concerned about being pregnant, but she went to the appointment anyway. After checking in with the receptionist, Vida was called into the back and blood was drawn. After waiting almost an hour, the fertility specialist entered the room. Vida looked at him blankly as he announced 'Sweetheart, you're pregnant!' Vida's mouth dropped open. She was in complete shock. 'I'm what?' she asked him. 'Pregnant!' he repeated. 'Aren't you happy?' he asked her. She was happy and terrified at the same time. She pretended to be happy for the doctor, but her heart was racing, her palms were sweating, and all she could think about was how many times she had unprotected sex with DJ. It was natural to have unprotected sex with her husband, but since she had allowed Marcus to convince her that she couldn't have kids she wasn't concerned with protecting herself from DJ."

Candice sat in wide-eyed wonder as Dr. Monroe told the story. She was captivated by all that was going on in the lives of complete strangers. She wanted to ask Dr. Monroe how he knew so much, but she took mental notes and decided to ask later. "Doc, you keep pausing and the suspense is killing me!" she said with a serious giggle.

"Well," he started again, "Vida decided to break it off with DJ. She wanted to work on her marriage because she felt like that was the right thing to do. She hoped that the baby belonged to Marcus, but decided either way, she wasn't going to tell DJ about the baby. DJ was heartbroken. He didn't understand why she was ending it, but he respected the fact that she wanted to give her marriage another try.

Vida went home to share the news with Marcus and was in for a rude awakening. Vida called Marcus into the living room and asked him to sit in front of her. She held both of his hands lovingly, stared into his dreamy eyes and shouted, 'We're going to have a baby!' Marcus stared at her with cold and empty eyes. Vida had never seen such a look in Marcus' eyes. 'Say something Marcus,' she said sadly to him. 'You're a lying bitch!' he yelled at her. Vida was shocked! 'How could you call me that?' she asked him. Marcus got close to Vida's face and whispered angrily, 'I had a vasectomy last year.' Marcus watched all of the blood drain from Vida's face. 'You were trying to have my baby and I was stopping you from ruining my life. I don't know who the lucky motherfucker is, but now you and your baby are his problem.' Marcus walked out of the house and left Vida sitting silently on the sofa. Vida went to bed hoping that everything that happened was a bad dream. She woke up in the morning with eleven missed calls and twenty-seven text messages on her phone. She read the messages and learned that Marcus told his family and her family about her affair and the illegitimate baby she was carrying. Vida knew what she did was wrong, but she didn't feel like she deserved what he did or those cruel messages. She was hurt and embarrassed. The only people she would talk to were her sisters. It was a really bad time for Vida. Marcus had moved out and she hadn't seen or heard from him since she told him about the baby. A couple of weeks had passed when Vida decided to call DJ. He ignored her calls and text messages so she decided to go to the gym. Vida walked in. It was evident that she had lost weight, but DJ noticed she didn't look healthy. She looked sad. She walked up to him slowly and asked for five minutes of his time. DJ didn't answer; he only stared at her. Vida could see the love, the hurt, and the hate in his eyes. 'DJ,' she said to him. It was as if he snapped out of the trance he was in. 'I don't have anything to say to you, Vida,' he said and he turned to walk away from her. Vida reached for him and pulled away. 'DJ, please,' she said with tears in her eyes, but he kept walking. 'I'm pregnant!' she yelled out and DJ stopped in his tracks. 'And it's yours,' she said. DJ's back was still turned towards her. DJ was stuck. His anger made him want to walk away from her, but she was carrying his child. His first child."

"Oh wow," Candice said with widened eyes. "Did he turn around, Doc?! Did he turn around?!" she said as she moved to the edge of her seat.

"DJ finally turned and looked at Vida. 'That's your husband's baby,' he said to her coldly. She told him that Marcus had a vasectomy, but DJ remained silent. Vida was dying from his silence, but he was all she had left. 'I have to go, Vida. I'll call you later.'

"That was cold-blooded!" Candice said.

"It was, but maybe that's what Vida needed at that time," Dr. Monroe said as he shrugged his shoulders.

"So what happened when he called her? Did he even call?" Candice asked.

"He never called and Vida was distraught."

"Bastard!" Candice yelled.

Dr. Monroe chuckled. "He showed up at her door a week later. Vida leaned in to kiss him and he stepped back. "

"He rejected her?" Candice asked.

"He did. He told her they needed to start over. He said, 'We need to start over, Vida. I want to be there for my child and I will be. I just don't trust you.' Vida was sad, but she understood his point and she was grateful for the second chance. Vida and DJ are still together to this day."

"That's so crazy," Candice said. "I'm really glad it worked out for her. But what happened to the other sisters?"

"I need you to understand that life will never be perfect for anyone," Dr. Monroe said to her. "With these stories I need you to see that even when your daughters don't make the best decisions, things can still turn our well for them. Now, please, will you allow me to finish the stories?"

Candice nodded her head. "Who's next?" She asked.

"Amanda," Dr. Monroe said. "Amanda was the quiet one of the three of them and she was a genius. They were identical, but she was shapelier than the others. No one could understand it, especially since she was a tomboy. She like to go fishing and motorcycle riding with their dad. He even talked her into Karate lessons and she was great at it."

"Really?" Candice asked, genuinely shocked.

"Really," he said. "She even became a blackbelt."

"Wow," Candice said.

"Amanda was the boy their dad always wanted," Dr. Monroe said with a chuckle. "Mandy was a perfectionist," he said.

"Mandy?"

"Oh yeah," that's what the family called her," Dr. Monroe said. "Whenever their dad, or anyone, showed her something, she perfected it. All she had to do was try whatever it was once or twice and it stuck with her. That's how she ended up with the black-belt in Karate. She ate, slept, and breathed Karate three days a week. She became bored with it around the age of fifteen so their dad let her quit. The family thinks that's what shaped her body that way. She went from having a body like a tomboy to having a body like Jessica Rabbit," he laughed.

"Jessica Rabbit?"

"Are you telling me you don't remember the movie *Roger Rabbit*?" Dr. Monroe asked in a shocked tone.

"Oh yeah. I guess I just didn't connect the dots. Wow. Jessica Rabbit was hot," she said.

"And so was Amanda, but while Jessica was devoted to Roger Rabbit, Amanda had a different boyfriend every weekend. Truth be told, she was a bit loose. Her sisters tried to reel her in, but she refused to listen to them. She told them that they were jealous of her. They were shocked and upset that she'd said that because the sisters were never in competition with one another. They were all awesome in their own right."

"Why did they care if she was a ho?" Candice asked. "What she did didn't affect them. They should have just let it go." Candice said with a shrug.

"I guess, but I think they were more disturbed by the fact that she was always dating losers. Her boyfriend at that time, Gavin, was beating on her."

"What?!" Candice said with widened eyes.

Dr. Monroe shrugged. "She denied it because she knew Kalila and Vida would tell their dad and Mr. Hudson was known to be a little on the crazy side. Especially when it came to his daughters."

"What do you think their dad would have done?" Candice asked.

"I'm certain Mr. Hudson would have killed Gavin," Dr. Monroe said with a straight face.

"Wow," Candice said. "So what happened with Gavin?"

"Before they had the chance to bring it up to her again, Gavin was a distant memory," he said with a shrug. "The sisters thought Amanda would slow down with dating so many men when she started college at Virginia Tech. They assumed that since she majored in Engineering and was on the basketball team that she wouldn't have time to date because she would be too busy studying and practicing with the team and on perfecting her game. Boy were they wrong! The sisters had gone home for winter and spring break, but Amanda didn't. When the sisters asked their parents, they were told that Amanda was focusing on her school work. Vida said every time she heard from Amanda she was partying. Ironically, Amanda finished her first year on the Dean's List. Her sisters had no idea how she did it and neither did anyone else. Her second year at Tech she started dating Terry. Terry was all she ever talked about. No one really cared to hear this Terry person because of Mandy's track record in relationships. This, however, was the first time Mandy had wanted her sisters to meet someone and they were shocked. They knew their sister was finally serious about someone.

When the sisters returned home for winter break, Amanda invited her sisters to a restaurant to meet Terry and they were happy to do so. When Vida and Kalila arrived at the restaurant, Amanda was hugged up with some girl.

"What!? Hugged up? With a girl?! Are you serious, Doc!?" Candice asked.

"I sure am. Mandy had started experimenting with women. So anyway, the sisters saw Terry and Mandy and Vida spoke first. 'Um, hey Mandy,' Vida said to her. 'Hey girls!' Amanda exclaimed. 'This is Terry!' Her sisters were completely shocked. Terry extended her hand to shake their hands, but neither of them moved. Mandy gave them the look of death and that snapped Kalila back to life. 'You look familiar,' Kalila managed to get out. 'She's one of my team members,' Amanda said with an attitude. Again, both sisters stared in shock. Terry and Mandy talked throughout lunch. Vida and Kalila were cordial, but they were sad. Vida cried as she drove back home. Vida and Kalila were concerned with Mandy's promiscuity. They never expected Mandy to add a woman to her list. The sisters later learned that Terry was just as violent as Gavin and Mandy was just as scared of her. Kalila and Vida decided it was time to get their parents involved."

"Wow, that had to be really hard for them," Candice said.

"It was, but it had to be done," Dr. Monroe said. "The sisters planned a family trip at Wintergreen. The trip doubled as an intervention site for Mandy because they couldn't seem to find time alone with her. Terry was always around. They were surprised to learn that Terry didn't insert herself onto the family trip. Amanda arrived two hours late and their mother was crying. Mandy thought someone had died. 'No one died,' Kalila said, 'but we would like for you to sit between mom and dad.' That made Amanda nervous. The sisters confronted her about her promiscuity with both men and women in front of their parents. They thought their sister would get up and leave, but surprisingly, she curled up on the sofa in the fetal position and cried unconsolably. When Mandy finally stopped crying, she shared some sad and scary things with her family."

"Like what?" Candice interrupted.

"Like how her Karate teacher had been molesting her for years," Dr. Monroe said.

"Oh my goodness!"

"Yeah. He told her that he would tell her parents that she came on to him and she actually believed him since she never said anything. The Karate teacher was a scumbag. It was interesting because they found his body in his office at the Dojo, or rather, the Karate school, with a bullet in his head. He must have messed with the wrong man's little girl and her father or someone went after him and killed him," Dr. Monroe shrugged.

"Wow," Candice said.

"Their father was angry. Their mother tried to console her, but she was beyond comfort at this point. She finally stood up and walked over to a corner in the room, sat down, and wrapped her arms around her legs. Her sisters tried to comfort her, but she waived them off. 'I'm ok,' she said. 'I won't be able to finish if you don't just let me be alone over here.' The sisters sat back down and let Amanda talk. She told the family about a few guys that had beat on her and the meaningless sex she used to try to heal from the abuse. She told them that she wasn't really in love with Terry, but that she'd had so many bad experiences with men that a woman had to be better. Unfortunately, Terry was just as abusive as the men she had dated. Kalila referred Mandy for counseling. Initially she was reluctant because she thought Kalila was trying to push her own agenda, but when the family pressed her about it, she gave in. It's a good thing too because Terry was prepared to propose to Mandy. If not for the intervention, she may have accepted. Amanda started going to counseling a few weeks later. Two years after the intervention, Mandy was very different. She had graduated from college with high honors and was working as a Systems Analyst for a Fortune 500 company. Amanda healed better than anyone expected. She eventually started dating a man named Charles. He and Amanda met one day after she left a therapy session. A few days after she and Charles met, she learned that Charles was seeking therapy at the same facility. He had been abused by both of his parents and wasn't able to maintain a functional relationship with anyone so he had never been married or had children. He just wanted to avoid people to keep from inflicting his internal pain on them. After hearing his story, Amanda was afraid to date him, but she could tell he simply needed friend and she knew that she could end a friendship easily if things didn't go well. They exchanged telephone numbers and started hanging out as friends. Neither of them ever discussed being in a relationship. They were enjoying the laughs, the conversations, and being in each other's presence. They became best friends and Charles was like a member of the family. One New Year's Eve, the family was home preparing for the ball to drop in Times Square in New York. They all sat around the television waiting for the new year to come in. 'Ten, nine, eight, seven... four, three, two, one – Happy New Year!' the family yelled in unison. Mandy turned to hug Charles and he was on one knee with a ring in his hand."

"Oh my gosh!" Candice exclaimed.

"Mandy was in shock. She stood in the living room with her hands covering her mouth. 'Amanda Hudson, you are my best friend. I have never loved anyone. You know everything about me so you know why. But I love you and I can't imagine my life without you. You are my world. Let me love you for the rest of our lives. Will you marry me?' Amanda was crying at this point. Kalila and Vida were standing there with their hands covering their mouths. No one wanted to say anything, but Vida couldn't resist. 'Say yes, dammit!' Everyone broke out into laughter except Amanda and Charles. Amanda took a deep breath and whispered, 'Yes.' 'Did she just say yes?' Kalila asked and looked around the room. 'Yes!' Amanda shouted. Charles stood up, grabbed Amanda by her waist, and lifted her into his arms. They kissed for the first time. Charles released Amanda to the floor then slid the ring onto her finger. They were married on Valentine's Day of that year," Dr. Monroe finished.

"They were engaged on New Year's and married by Valentine's Day of the same year?" Candice asked.

"Yes, they were."

"Wow. That's beautiful," Candice said. "Ok, ok, ok! Tell me about Kalila!" Candice said with excitement.

Dr. Monroe laughed. "Are you sure you want to hear that story?" he asked jokingly.

"Doc! Cut it out!"

"Ok, ok, ok," Dr. Monroe said. "Kalila was the free spirit. She loved her sisters, but she liked to do things on her own. Strangely enough, she had never left home until senior year of high school. Her summer before college, Kalila went to the Beachfest in Fort Lauderdale. While there she met this amazing, but damaged guy named Raffiel."

Candice laughed. "Is it funny telling a story about a guy with the same name as your own?"

Dr. Monroe smiled. "Not at all. Raffiel met Kalila at one of the Beachfest parties. At the time, Raffiel was living in Charlottesville and Kalila was living in Hampton, Virginia, but neither of them knew it. They were focused on the coincidence that they met in Florida and both of them were headed to Florida State University. Kalila majored in Sociology with a focus on Social Work and Counseling. It worked well for her because she was great with people. Let's rewind to Kalila's college years. Kalila was excited to attend Florida State. Going away to college was only her second time being away and she had never been more excited. She moved into the dorms a day early. Her suitemate, Katelyn, didn't arrive until the following day. Kalila was happy to be alone to enjoy the peace and quiet for the night. Katelyn arrived the next morning and all Kalila could wonder was why was she so early. Kalila got out of bed, put on her bathrobe, introduced herself. 'I'm Kalila, how are you?' she asked as she yawned. Katelyn giggled. 'I'm Katelyn,' she said, 'but everyone calls me Katie." Katelyn was beautiful, just like her parents. Each of them looked as if they'd just walked off the centerfold of a beauty and fashion magazine. They were rich and you could see it all over them. Katelyn's parents took the girls out that night. Kalila believed that that Katelyn's parents wanted to check out their daughter's rich roommate. Kalila didn't mind though. She appreciated the kind gesture. Months later, Kalila grew to appreciate Katie. She kept her side of the room clean, she kept to herself, but she was cool with everyone. Katie and Kalila went to the dining hall together daily, attended campus parties together, and studied together.

Kalila valued her friendship. Kalila was open to knowing everyone, but Katie was drawn to the wealthy guys. Most of the guys she knew drove G-Wagons to school every day. 'How in the world does a freshman drive a G-Wagon?' Kalila asked. 'Most of them received them as graduation gifts,' she answered. 'You don't have a car?' Katie asked. 'It was never really necessary,' she answered with a shrug. 'It's cool,' Katie said with a smile. Kalila and Katie were invited to a big party outside of the school. They received VIP, all-access passes to a club called The Moon. Kalila was gorgeous in her tight, white, sleeveless dress and orange Louboutin strap-up shoes. She later realized that those shoes were made simply for standing in place and not for walking," he said with a laugh.

Dr. Monroe stopped talking for a moment and stared off towards the window.

"You ok, Doc?" Candice asked.

"Yeah, I'm fine. So, anyway, someone tapped Kalila on her bare shoulder. She turned around and he watched as the curls on the side of head swept over her shoulder. She was just as beautiful as he remembered. It was Raffiel. The handsome and amazing guy she met the summer of her senior year. 'Kalila, hey!' he said to her. 'Raffiel? I can't believe you remember me.' 'I could never forget a woman so beautiful,' he said to her. Kalila let Katie know that she was going to the twenty-four-hour campus coffee house with Raffiel and that she would be home late. They arrived at Raffiel's vehicle and Kalila couldn't help but to wonder if Mercedes had a fifty-percent off sale on G-wagons because way too many students at Florida State drove them."

Candice laughed out loud.

"They spent the entire night talking and laughing. They talked about school, scholarships, family and all types of things. Realizing they were both from Virginia, Kalila wanted to know why Raffiel didn't go to school closer to home. 'I wanted to be far from home,' he shared. Raffiel giggled. 'What's so funny?' Kalila asked. 'Don't think I'm crazy or that I'm a stalker, but I Googled you when we met at the Beachfest.' 'You did what?' she asked with a laugh. 'I'll do you one better,' he said to her as he pulled his phone out of his pocket. Raffiel showed her a picture of herself and her eyes expanded. 'Oh my goodness!' she said and broke out laughing. Raffiel showed her a photo where she had braces, neon rubber bands, knobbed knees, and bushy eyebrows. Her knees and head were the biggest things on her, but even in that photo he could see that she was beautiful. He was impressed with Kalila and he didn't want their conversation to end. They continued to talk when a waitress came by the table, excused herself, and exchanged the dinner menu for the breakfast menu. 'Oh my goodness,' Kalila said. 'It's daylight.' Raffiel smiled. 'I really need to go,' she said. 'I know.' Raffiel took her back to her dorm. He walked her to her room. 'May I take you to your classes tomorrow?' he asked. 'Sure,' she said shyly. She told him her schedule and he laughed. 'What's funny?' she asked. 'I have all of those classes at those exact same times!' They shared a laugh. 'You really are a Social Work major!' she said with a laugh. Raffiel fell deeply in love with Kalila and she did the same. If they weren't in class they were studying together or spending time at the coffee house or on dates. They enjoyed one another and it was nice," Dr. Monroe said. "Track meets kept Raffiel pretty busy. Kalila attended most of his events, but kept herself busy with running for exercise, hot yoga, and volunteering at the local food bank. One of Kalila's professors recognized her compassion and love for helping people and suggested she volunteer at a woman's shelter. Working there was an eye-opener for her. All of the women there had been physically or verbally abused in relationships. Kalila knew her parents' marriage wasn't perfect, but she also knew there was never any physical or verbal abuse between them. Kalila was able to empathize with the women at the shelter even though she never experienced what they had. People always told her that was a gift she had. Her mission was to help as many women as she could realize their self-worth and to walk in their greatness. While working with the women, Kalila realized that women's counseling and empowerment was her spiritual calling. She spent so much time at the shelter she stopped volunteering at the foodbank. Raffiel and Kalila's relationship grew and deepened. There was trust, understanding, and respect, and they both loved it. Raffiel eventually took an internship with the Village Ministries. Village Ministries was founded by Stephen

Foster, one of his childhood friends. The organization was primarily counseling based, but the therapists used their expertise to mentor young men who were raised by single mothers. The ministry also offered housing services for disabled men. The company was person-centered and did a lot for the community. Raffiel really enjoyed working with the ministry. He would always say, 'Reach one teach one.'"

"Oh, that's cool Doc. You always say that too."

Dr. Monroe smiled. "Raffiel and Kalila wanted to marry one another, but they felt like they needed to finish college first and they were too young. Raffiel also had secrets."

"Secrets?" Candice asked.

Dr. Monroe nodded. "Raffiel was raised with both parents in the home, but he suffered with low self-esteem. They tried to buy him and his brother because they never had time for their children. I guess that was good though because his father was verbally and physically abusive to him and his brother. Raffiel received the most abuse. No one really knew why, but they assumed it was because Raffiel was the oldest. His father constantly referred to him as 'sissy boy." Raffiel eventually learned that the abuse was hereditary. His grandfather was an alcoholic and abused his father. When he was old enough, Raffiel's father ran away from home and stayed with his Aunt Grace. Raffiel's mother was afraid of his father. The family's money was because of his mother. She was afraid to stop the abuse, but she made sure her boys didn't want for anything, hence the G-Wagon he drove. Raffiel and Kalila married about a year after college. They both secured great jobs, but the demons of Raffiel's past began to surface. Their college relationship was perfect, but their marriage started off kind of rocky. Kalila spent a lot of time trying to reassure Raffiel and it was emotionally draining. Kalila, at some point, even felt defeated. She was able to build the women at the women's shelter, but no matter what she did, she couldn't heal her husband. Her job was to point out his wonderful attributes, but he didn't believe it about himself. The abuse he endured at the hands of his father was overwhelming and it stripped him of his self-worth. Raffiel was a counselor, but struggled with receiving counseling because he was so closed off. He finally agreed to seek individual counseling and he and Kalila went to marriage counseling. At some point Kalila thought it was important that the counselors were Christian. Working at the shelter she seemed to realize that the spiritual component better helped with the healing. Counseling worked better than either of them expected. Raffiel had a newfound confidence which not only made him a better person and husband; it made him a better counselor."

"What an amazing story," Candice said. "Whatever happened to Raffiel's father?"

Raffiel's cellphone rang before he could answer Candice's question. He looked at the phone and smiled.

"Excuse me," he said to Candice. Hello," he said in a loving tone. "Yes, I'm ready. I'm just finishing up with a client. Ok. I'll be ready when you arrive. I love you too. Bye-bye."

"I'm sorry about that. It was my wife," he said.

"No problem," she said. "So, Doc, what happened to Raffiel's father?"

"Oh, I'm glad you asked, Candice," he said. "Raffiel's father ended up having a stroke and guess who was left to take care of him?"

"Raffiel," Candice said sadly. "That must have been hard considering how cruel his father was to him."

"It was, but thankfully, his Christian counselor reminded him of the importance of forgiving himself as well as those who hurt us. Raffiel spent a lot of time in Charlottesville with his father. Someone else may have hired a nurse to come in and help, but Raffiel went home and took care of both of his parents. Raffiel's father called him a sissy boy all of his life. Those tender qualities were what helped his father during his time of need. Life with Raffiel and Kalila wasn't perfect, but it got better every day."

"Doc," Candice started, "that was an amazing story. It was really encouraging. I get it. I have to let my girls just go through the motions but pay attention to signs of anything strange with them."

"Exactly!" he said and stood up from his chair. "You would be amazed at how things work out if you just let them play themselves out."

"Thanks, Doc," Candice said as she stood up.

There was a knock at the door.

"Come in," he shouted across the room.

"Hey honey," the beautiful woman said as she entered the office. "Oh, I'm sorry. I thought you were alone," she said.

"It's fine. Honey, this is Candice. Her twin daughters frequent the center."

His wife reached out her hand to shake Candice's hand.

"Forgive my husband. All of those smarts make him forget that I actually have a name. My name is Kalila Monroe," she said and flashed perfect white teeth.

Candice's eyes widened as she put two and two together. "Kalila as in Raffiel and Kalila?!" she asked.

Kalila looked at her husband strangely and Dr. Monroe broke out into laughter. He pulled two photos from his bookcase and handed them to Candice.

"Yes, Candice, I am the Raffiel in the story and this is the beauty of the triplets," he said and hugged his wife.

"Did you tell our stories again?" she asked and hit him playfully on his arm.

"I did, but she needed it," he said with a smile. "Candice has twin daughters that are a mixture of you, Vida, and Amanda."

Kalila smiled and walked over to Candice. She hugged her tightly and Candice started to cry. Kalila handed her a tissue from the box on Raffiel's desk. "Candice, I don't know you, but the fact that my husband told you that story shows that you are an amazing mom and you're on the right track. Don't second guess yourself. Continue to love on your girls and trust your instincts."

"Thank you," Candice said. "Thank you both." She took another tissue from the box on the desk and left the room.

"I am so proud of you," Kalila said to Raffiel. "I don't know how I got so lucky to end up with you."

Raffiel smiled and wrapped his arms tightly around his wife. "Well, if you don't know, you're going to learn today."

The couple shared a laugh, kissed lightly, then left his office.

CHAPTER 12
REVEREND LEE

I'm not bragging, but I'm one of those CME Christians. You know... those people that go to church on Christmas, Mother's Day, and Easter – hence the acronym "CME." Again, I'm not proud of the designation, but it's what I am. It's been two years since I've been home and probably longer since I attended church, but mother asked me to come back home to Memphis this year. I figured since the visit was around Mother's Day, I'd go to church with her. I knew she would like that. I had to go out and purchase something church appropriate to attend service. It wasn't that I didn't have anything appropriate, but mother is kind of old school and I'm sure she wouldn't approve of any skirt or dress that sat above my knees.

It was unseasonably hot for this time of year. I don't remember it being this hot when I was growing up. I took a taxi to the house and he had the windows rolled down which didn't help at all. It was just hot air blowing into my face. I guess I could have asked mother to pick me up, but I needed to get my mind right before seeing her. She could be a little excessive at times.

In mother-like fashion, as soon as I arrived at the house, she reminded me about Sunday service.

"I hope you brought something suitable to wear on Sunday," she said.

"I did," I said, knowing she was expecting a response.

"Are you being sarcastic with me Camille Vivian Hopson?"

"Oh no, mother," I answered. I wasn't being sarcastic; I just knew what was coming. Just like the next question.

"So, when are you going to settle down?" she asked.

I ignored that question.

"We can talk about that after I've washed the travel dirt off of me," I said with a giggle.

She gave me a look. She knew I was avoiding that conversation. Mothers can almost always tell. To be perfectly honest, I had no idea when I was going to get serious with anyone. I always felt like my soulmate had to meet the "Money, Power, Respect" requirements for me to even consider settling down with him. Yes, he had to have all three: money, power, and respect. I was currently dating three MPRs. There was a congressman, a physician, and an officer in the Air Force all waiting for me back at home.

Mother and I spent the day just relaxing and catching up on life when I felt myself becoming tired.

"I'm going to bed now, mother. Do you need anything before I turn in?" I asked her.

"No dear, I'm fine. You go on to bed. We'll talk more in the morning," she answered.

"Pumpkin, wake up," mother said softly. "We have to get ready for church."

I rolled over to my mother's smiling face. "Some things never change," I thought as I smiled up at my mother. She still calls me Pumpkin, even as a grown woman, and she still wakes up at the butt crack of dawn for no reason.

"Mother," I said before she left the room.
"Yes, dear," she answered.

"Why are you always up so early?" I asked with a yawn.

She smiled. "Your father used to have to be to work early so I always got up with him. We would pray together, I would have his lunch prepared, then he would kiss me goodbye. I guess old habits just die hard. Now, instead of spending my morning time with your father, I spend time with our heavenly Father."

She never ceased to amaze me. I never knew that about them. I just thought she couldn't sleep.

Mom and dad were very active at Living Waters Baptist Church and had been members for twenty-five years. Mother was a deaconess and my father was a trustee. Everyone knew Dr. and Mrs. Randolph Hopson.   Dad used to attend church with us as often as possible after the prostate cancer worsened. Mother watched as her active husband slowed down until prostate cancer won the battle and took his life nine years ago. I really miss him when I'm home. I think that's kind of the reason I don't come home too often.

I remember being in church all day every Sunday, so when I left home that was over. It wasn't that I didn't like church, I just didn't think I needed to be sitting up in church all day every Sunday. I preferred to spend my Sundays lying down. Preferably with one of my MPR men. If mother knew I was attending "Bedside Baptist" every Sunday she would keel over.

I showered and dressed for church. As I was getting dressed the aroma of breakfast crept up the stairs. I came downstairs to the best breakfast this side of heaven. My mother made homemade sweet potato pancakes with honey butter syrup, scrambled eggs, and was slicing fresh fruit when I entered the kitchen. My mouth watered as I sat down and placed a napkin on my lap.

Mother and I used this time before church to have girl talk. At least that's what we liked to call the church gossip. She told me the church currently had 3,000 members and I almost spit out my coffee.

"Three thousand?!" I said shocked.

"Yes, ma'am. We doin' it big now," she joked as she sipped her coffee.

"No disrespect, but the church is the size of a Cracker Jack box. How in the world do you fit that many members?" I asked.

She went on to explain that the church had a new pastor, Reverend Ralston Lee. When he arrived, he had all kinds of fundraisers and within two years the congregation had saved enough money to buy a free-standing building. I remember when she complained about having to leave an hour early just to get a parking space and now the church was hosting gospel concerts for big name stars.

"You can't be serious! Name some of the artists mother," I said and waited.

She pulled out some of the programs from her drawer. Ty Tribbett, Israel Houghton, just to name a couple. Joyce Meyers had even done a free show there. I couldn't wait to see this new church.

"And Camille," she started with a giggle, "the pastor is fine!"

I broke out into laughter. "What you mean *fine*? I'm sure our definitions are very different!"

"Trust me, our definitions are the same. Wait until you see him. Come on now, finish up. I don't want to be late," she said as she stood to take her plate to the sink.

I volunteered to drive because my mother was a real live Sunday driver. She drove with her hands at the standardized "10 & 2" and for some reason she drove ten miles under the speed limit. I also wanted to spoil her. She was always a great mother to me and loving and caring to others. I wanted her to feel special, especially on Mother's Day.

I saw this stadium like structure as we exited the freeway, but didn't give it much thought.

"There it is," mother said proudly.

My eyes widened. "What?! Are you serious!?"

"I sure am," she said as she crossed her arms proudly.

This church was very different from the fish-dinner selling, tent revival celebrating structure I attended as a young girl. We sold fish dinners and desserts and had garage sales just to raise money for choir robes and now I'm driving into a parking lot filled with luxury vehicles.

"This is right up my MPR alley," I thought to myself with a smile.

We had great seats. It was clear that mother was still very well respected in the congregation. Everyone greeted her with warm hugs, handshakes, and smiles as they came in.

"This is my daughter, Camille," she would say as she introduced me.

"Little Camille, oh my goodness!" Some of them said.

Some I remembered, others I would rather have forgotten. Like old Mr. Dandy. He was always offering us candy. We always thought he was a dirty old man and called him "Dirty Dandy". I felt the same way when he reached in to hug me. I leaned back and held out my hand.

"You will not hug on me Dirty Dandy," I thought to myself.

The praise and worship portion of service was out of this world! I couldn't remember the last time I felt so moved during a church service. The pastor and his wife, Lady Laurie, entered shortly after praise and worship.

"That's the pastor," mother whispered to me.

My heart skipped a beat and my panties got moist when I saw him. "Damn," I thought to myself. "Oops, excuse me Lord," I couldn't catch myself fast enough.

I was almost embarrassed because of those thoughts, but the fact of the matter is that he may be a pastor but clearly, he was all man. Mother was right when she said he was fine.

The picture on the program didn't do him any justice. The picture had to be about ten years old, if not older. Pastor Lee was fair-skinned and tall. He had dark features: dark eyebrows, a dark mustache, and jet-black hair. He put me in the mind of an older Omari Hardwick. Pastor Lee knew he was fine as hell. His suit was cut to show off his well-defined torso and his muscular arms.

"Get yourself together, Cammie," I thought. I found myself fanning myself and I wasn't even hot! Pastor Lee had definitely lit a fire beneath me though. "Hell has a front row seat with your name on it. Girl, pray and get your hormones under control!" I couldn't keep my thoughts on the service.

I couldn't imagine how hard it had to be for his wife. All these females lusting for her husband, including me.

Pastor Lee definitely met the MPR criteria. I saw the Range Rover HSE in the Pastor's parking space of the lot. Lady Lee was fly too, in a churchy kind of way. I tried to contain the lust that kept welling up inside of me, but I couldn't stop it. I don't even remember what the sermon was about! Hell, I didn't even realize he had started preaching.

I wanted to say service was amazing, but I spent the entire service reading scripture trying to contain my hormones. Mother took me downstairs to meet Pastor and Lady Lee. God, how I wish she wouldn't have done that.

"Pastor and Lady Laurie, this is my daughter, Cammie," she said with her informal introduction.

"Camille," I corrected politely.

As soon as my hand touch his it felt like I had been struck by a bolt of lightning.   He felt it too; I could see it in his eyes.

"Are you going to attend the Mother's Day Luncheon in the fellowship hall?" Lady Laurie asked.

I looked at my mother for confirmation and she nodded affirmatively. That was a great idea because I was not in the mood to sit anywhere waiting for a seat because they wouldn't accept holiday reservations.

When I opened the doors of the fellowship hall I had to put my eyes back in my head. I was astounded. That place looked like a room in the White House.

"Where were the fold-up funeral home chairs and wooden paneling on the walls?" I asked myself as I slowly admired the furnishings. As we were waiting to be seated my mother asked if I enjoyed the service. I didn't respond.

"Pumpkin," she started, "what are you over there thinking about?"

"I'm sorry, what did you say mother?"

"Did you enjoy service?" she repeated.

"Oh, yeah! Service was great!" Clearly, I lied because I was too busy trying to control my hormones. "Mother I am truly impressed with the growth of the church."

She smiled proudly.

"Seriously," I said. "There is nothing more disappointing then to come back to your childhood church to see that little picture of the church which shows there is still money needed for the building fund. I am very pleased," I said as I continued to look around. "Reverend Lee mentioned that the church was opening a transitional center for the homeless. I am very interested in making a donation to that cause."

"Oh, Pumpkin that would be great!"

Mother was beaming with joy. I was still lusting over Pastor Lee.

Lord, help me.

The brunch was fantastic. I'm not too fond of buffet style meals because everything seems so rushed, but this was very different. The Men's Ministry showed out for the Mother's Day Luncheon. I can't begin to imagine how much they paid for this spread. There was baked and fried chicken, fried oysters, there was a steamship round, baked flounder, Maryland crab cakes, assorted vegetables, and several desserts. Thankfully there was no formal program so it was just great food and great fellowship. I really enjoyed this time with mother.

Reverend Lee and Lady Laurie stood to give closing remarks when the luncheon was coming to an end. For just a moment I had my thoughts under control and my undies were no longer moist. I was back to praying for self-control and strength. I did not want to see him again.

The guests clapped after the remarks were completed and mother called Reverend Lee over to the table.

"Hello again Sister Hopson! And happy Mother's Day! I'm sorry, I don't think I said it earlier when we spoke," he said.

"Oh, it's fine Pastor Lee. I just wanted to tell you that my Cammie wants to contribute to the transitional center.

Pastor Lee looked at me and smiled with his pretty, white teeth.

"She's going to write a big check," she said proudly. "Isn't that right Cammie?"

I smiled. Mostly because I was trying to control my thoughts.

"Oh, what a blessing," he said. "Since it's a new program, we're also hiring for management positions if you're interested."

"I'm just visiting, but thank you. I live in Houston and my employer pays me pretty well," I said.

"What kind of work do you do?" he asked.

"Lord, why won't this fine, married man just walk away from me?" I thought to myself.

"I'm a nurse practitioner," I answered.

"That's great! We're hiring medical staff too," he said.

"That's nice to know," I said with a smile.

I just wanted him to keep it moving at this point before a puddle formed at my ankles. The moisture was now out of control.

"Excuse me," I said, "I need to get my checkbook." My checkbook was right in my pocketbook, but I needed to be away from him and that sexy smelling cologne.

I went to another room and wrote a check for five-thousand dollars.

"This will be a great tax deduction," I thought to myself.

I returned and handed the check to Reverend Lee.

"Praise God!" he shouted.

Lady Laurie walked over. "Yes! What has God done now?" She asked in an excited tone.

He showed her the check and she gave me a big hug. "Praise God!" She said. "Is this your correct address? I'm asking so we can mail you the tax form for the deduction."

"Yes, it's correct." I answered.

Mother and I headed home full and sleepy. "Ten, nine, eight, seven..."

"Pumpkin," she started.

I giggled quietly. "If you must know, mother, I donated five-thousand dollars."

Mother laughed out loud. "How did you know I was going to ask you that?"

We were both laughing now. "I know you very well, mother."

"That job in Houston must be paying you very well!" She said.

"Yes, it does, mother."

"Thank you for the donation, Pumpkin."

"It was my pleasure," I answered. In my mind I was thinking my job pays me well, but I used the twenty-five hundred dollars that Dr. Kyle gave me for spending money.

Mother and I stayed up talking until ten o'clock that night.

"I need to go shower and pack now. I need to be at airport by 4am."

"Ok Pumpkin. Sleep well," mother said. She kissed me on my forehead and we went upstairs.

Mother made sure I was awake the next morning. I smelled breakfast once again.

"Mother its three-fifteen in the morning. What could you possibly have cooked so early?" I said with a giggle.

"It's just a breakfast burrito," she said with a smile.

She handed the wrapped-up breakfast meal to me and kissed my forehead.

I smiled and hugged my mother. I love her so much.

The taxi was right on schedule. I gave mother another big hug and a kiss.

"I'll call as soon as I get home, mother."

"Ok Pumpkin."

Dr. Kyle picked me up from the airport. I was actually kind of happy to see him. Of all the MPRs, Dr. Kyle was the sweetest. I think he loved me, but he had never said it. I was ready to go home and relax, but he wanted to take me back to his place. I was fine with spending time there, but didn't realize he was more interested in intense love making. Poor Dr. Kyle. He had no idea he was going to be replaced by Reverend Lee in my mind. I know that's wrong, but I couldn't shake my desire for that man.

"Girl, that was out of this world," he said as he tried to catch his breath. "You need to go visit your mother more often!" He said with a laugh.

"Ha, ha," I started, "you are so funny."

It felt so good to be home. I put my bags away and took a nice, hot bubble bath. As I laid in the fullness of the foam, my mind shifted to Reverend Lee. I tried to think negative thoughts about him to get my mind off of him.

"He probably has foul body odor and a small penis," I said with a giggle. Then I remembered that his cologne hypnotized me. "I can't do this." I got out of the bathtub and thought about my caseload for the next day. I had occupational physicals to complete, patient care plans to create, and I had to analyze diagnostic tests. I was tired just thinking about it.

I laid in bed in the darkness of my bedroom, but I still couldn't settle my mind. Work was a daily task, but so were the MPRs. I had a date with Major James Daniels after work. I wished I hadn't accepted the dinner date because he talked too damn much. I enjoyed every restaurant he took me to and he was never stingy with his money, but when I was ready to streamline the MPR crew, he would be the first to go!

I worked 12-hour shifts for the past four weeks and I was beat! I haven't had time for any dates since the last one with Major Daniels. Occasionally, I had dreams about Reverend Lee. Thankfully, he was miles away. I was finally home and able to just do nothing when I realized that I hadn't done my laundry. It had been piling up since I returned from Memphis. I tried to keep myself busy with household chores until the phone rang.

"A welcome distraction," I thought.

"Hello mother," I said. That was the only call I was going to accept. "How are you doing?"

"Hey Pumpkin I fell down the front steps when I went outside to check the mail."

"What? Are you ok?!" I asked frantically.

"No, I have to have surgery on my hip," she answered.

"For what day and time is the surgery scheduled?" I asked.

"Next Friday."

"No problem. I will be there on Thursday morning," I said.

"You don't need to come here, Pumpkin. I'll be fine."

I ignored her. "I'll be there on Thursday, mother. I want to speak to the orthopedic doctor for details."

"Ok, Pumpkin. I'll see you then," she said and we ended the call.

I was back in Memphis and it was hotter now then it was in May. I spoke with the doctor and was informed that her rehabilitation time would be four to six weeks as I expected. I was glad to have put in the FMLA request before I left Houston. I wasn't even concerned about the approval. I only had one mother and I was going to be where she needed me to be for as long as I needed to be there.

Mother's surgery went well and I received an email from Human Resources approving the FMLA request. I had plenty of vacation time to cover the time off, but I was thankful that it was one less thing I needed to think about while caring for mother.

Mother was sent to a community rehabilitation center in Memphis, but I was not having that. I had her transferred to the five-star, state of the art rehabilitation center located in downtown Memphis. It was expensive, but what her insurance didn't cover, I covered with the help of the Dr. Kyle MPR fund that I kept on reserve.

Mother was doing very well in her rehab. The problem was that she had too many visitors. Reverend Lee was her first visitor.

"Lord, help me," I said when he walked into the room.

"Good morning Sister Hopson," he addressed mother, "Cammie," then me as he flashed those white teeth.

"Good morning Pastor!" mother said joyfully.

"Good morning," I said. "You're looking pretty sharp in that Gucci ensemble," I said to him.

"Oh, you peeped that, huh?" He said with a sly smile.

"I did. Fashion is my thing. Low-key fashion is even nicer," I said. "And pricier," I thought to myself. "MPR. Check, check, and check. All requirements met."

"May I pray with you sister?" he asked as he reached for my mother's hand and broke into my impure thoughts.

"Of course, Pastor."

He reached for my hand and I wanted to pull away. I was going to need additional prayer because I was on the verge of an anxiety attack.

"I'm going to step out to make some calls so you can visit, Pastor. I'll be back mother," I said as I excused myself.

I returned to the room and he was still there. "Mother, I'm going to go to the cafeteria to get something to eat. I'll be right back."

"Sister Camille, may I join you?"

"Hell no!" I said to myself. "Sure," I replied.

We walked to the cafeteria in silence. I didn't want profane or sexual words to fall from my lips so I said nothing. He broke the silence in the elevator.

"Is everything ok back in Houston?"

"Yes, everything is fine. I just needed to call my job and see about my FMLA approval."

We ordered salads and water and sat down at a table near a window overlooking downtown Memphis.

"So what's up? I know you didn't want to just have lunch with me," even though I was hoping he did, "what's going on?" I asked seriously.

"I like a woman that's to the point," he said.

"This is a test. This is a test. This is a test and I can't fail," I thought to myself. I didn't respond.

He smiled. "Your mother's health is changing."

"Changing?" I interrupted.

"Possibly declining," he said seriously. "Did she tell you she hit three cars in the church parking lot within the past couple of weeks?"

"No, she didn't tell me that," I said with tears in my eyes.

He changed seats and sat beside me. He handed me a napkin from the dispenser and rubbed my shoulder to try to comfort me, but that didn't help. I knew I would have to make some life changes and quickly to be sure mother was taken care of.

"I'm going to move back to Memphis to take care of my mother."

"That may be very helpful," he said sincerely.

"Pastor, is the transitional center still looking for medical personnel? I'm going to need a job."

"Let me make a phone call," he said as he pulled out his cell phone and stepped away.

Pastor Lee returned a few minutes later. "It's settled, Camille. The HR Manager, Janine, will meet with you on Monday."

I sighed in relief and Reverend Lee had a big smile on his face.

"Is everything alright reverend?" I asked.

"Everything is fine. I just like delivering good news to people."

"What news is that?" I asked.

"I mentioned to Janine that your current employer paid you well..." he started.

"Reverend, I know that I will not make the same amount of money as I did in Houston. I'm really only concerned about taking care of my mother..."

"Sister Camille," he interrupted. "Relax," he said and touched my hand. "We may be able to get you very close to your current salary," he said.

"You won't be sorry! I'm great at what I do and I'm a hard worker. Thank you so much!" I said and squeezed his hand with both of my hands.

Pastor Lee stood to leave and I sat in the cafeteria thinking about my next move. I returned to mother's room and told her I needed to leave to go to the mall.

"You're going shopping?" she asked sadly.

"I need a suit. I have an interview at the transition center on Monday," I started.

"An interview?" She asked.

"Yes, mother. I'm moving back home."

Mother covered her mouth and cried. I hugged her, gave her a tissue, then left the room. It didn't take much to bring out those tears of joy.

"If I didn't know any better, I would think the good reverend only hired pretty women to work in this center," I thought to myself. All of the women were beautiful and fit. I felt like I had just stepped on the set of a Ms. Black America Pageant. Call me insecure, but if I were Lady Laurie, I would hire a center full of old maids.

Janine sent the receptionist to bring me to her office in the back of the center. This place was really nice. It was obvious the place was decorated by professionals. Every room had its own color scheme and seemed to encourage positivity. It was furnished with eclectic home and office pieces that gave it a professional, yet home-like feeling. Individuals that needed assistance would probably feel at home and at peace in each of the rooms. The decorator was very clever in the design.

I entered Janine's office and was blown away.

"Who the hell decorated this office and how much did it cost?" I wondered. It was evident that Reverend Lee spared no cost when it came to the comfort of his employees.

Janine was absolutely stunning and she greeted me with her

beautiful smile. She dressed like a runway model and her hair was perfect. We shook hands and she offered me a seat in a leather, cream and gold chair that faced her desk.

"Welcome to Memphis, Camille!"

"Thank you!" I wasn't expecting her to be so pleasant.

I scanned her desk as she flipped through my paperwork and began talking about the center.

"Your salary will be $125,000 per year. Reverend Lee told me to be competitive so we started you at the high end of the spectrum," she said. "I know that's a little lower than what you're making in Houston, but we're just starting out in this center and we have to pay modestly to start."

"Thank you, Reverend Lee," I said to myself. "That's fine. I knew I would take a pay cut. I'd do anything for my mother," I said to her.

"Yes, he told me that you were relocating for her. That is so admirable."

I smiled and signed my offer letter. Janine continued going over my responsibilities at the center and I explained that I had to give official notice at my job, return to Houston for a few days, then come back to Memphis. She was fine with my decisions and accepted that I would be able to officially start in about two weeks.

I stood and thanked her for her time and she gave me the once over. I don't think she realized that I caught that, but I'm a woman, we always catch it.

"Ok, Camille, I'll see you in a couple of weeks."

I returned to the hospital after the meeting with Janine and informed mother that I had accepted the position and would be leaving Memphis to arrange for movers to move things to Houston and to a storage unit until I got settled.

Major "Mouth All Mighty" picked me up from the airport. He was the first to receive the news of my move. I could tell he was sad, but I wasn't really bothered by it. He put my luggage down and handed me a gift.

"What is this James?"

"I know you've had your eye on this for a long time," and he handed me a wrapped box.

I unwrapped it and saw a George Forman grill box.

"What the hell..."

James broke out into laughter. I rolled my eyes.

"Cammie, just open the box," he said as he continued to laugh.

I opened the box to see an Alexander McQueen duffle bag for my frequent trips to Memphis and an Alexander McQueen trench coat just because he thought it be nice to add to my professional wardrobe. That earned James two hours of intense love making. I was satisfied so I had to make sure he was as well.

The following day I broke the news to Dr. Kyle and Congressman Milton Pulley. Kyle was sad and that actually bothered me a bit. The congressman didn't seem to care. I told them both I would stay in touch. I knew that was probably the end with the congressman, but I did kind of like Dr. Kyle. He was good to me and he was a passionate man.

My first day at work was really slow. I completed physicals and care plans on each patient. The task was pretty extensive because many of them hadn't seen a doctor in years. The following week, I was in a groove and the tasks, though similar in the sense that they were all new patients, were different because they all had a backstory that required different treatments. Sometimes I was treating the body; other days I was treating the mind.

Reverend Lee came by to check on me the following week.

"Your mother told me she would be getting out of rehab in about two weeks."

"Yes," I started. "God is good. She's healing a lot faster than they expected."

"I'm sure she is," he started. "Having you back home has motivated her."

I smiled.

"Have you found a place yet?" he asked.

"No, I'll be staying with mother for a few months to make sure she has all she needs. I also don't want her driving around too much. I just want to keep a close eye on her for a bit."

"I understand," he said. "It seems like the job is suiting you."

"It has! It's been great! I get personal satisfaction knowing I can help others, especially the less fortunate."

"Please let me know if your mother needs anything. She's been very supportive of me since I became the pastor."

"Ok, thanks again, Reverend Lee."

In the 15 minutes I spoke with the pastor, about five women walked back and forth past the office. I understood if Lady Laurie had women watching her man, but there was something very different about these looks. Pastor Lee was fine, but my mind wasn't there at this moment.

Janine invited me to lunch and I graciously accepted. I wasn't used to having female friends, but I figured I would give this a try. We went to a restaurant called Scrumptious. I learned that it was owned by the church and they serve organic soul food. I couldn't wait to try it out. I also wanted to get some information about the who's and the what's of the church and this new pastor.

Lunch with Janine was nothing like I expected. The food was delicious and I expected that I would visit there at least once a week, but instead of a gossip session with Janine, it was more like an interrogation.

"What made you move to Memphis?" That was weird because we discussed that on my interview day. "Are you married? Engaged? Seeing anyone? Anything serious? Any local prospects? What's your type? Have you ever been with a woman?"

"What the hell?!" I thought to myself. I was so confused! The reverent was fine and all, but I wasn't going there. I was attracted to him, but mother's condition caused me to refocus and he was no longer at the center of my thoughts. Janine was obviously Lady Laurie's spy and she was putting in work! Note to self, never go out to lunch – or anywhere else – with Janine again.

It was good to see mother up and out of the hospital.

"How are you feeling, mother?" I asked as she made herself comfortable on the sofa.

"I'm ok, Pumpkin. I don't need you fussing over me."

I smiled at her. I'm always going to fuss over her. My mother has been my biggest supporter and she deserved all of the love and care I could provide to her.

"Your church buddies are going to be very excited to see you tomorrow."

"I miss being in service. I'm excited to go back."

"I'll be there with you tomorrow, but you know I won't be there next week. That's moving weekend," I said excitedly.

"Oh, that's right! I'm so glad you're back! I can't wait for us to start spending time together again after I'm fully healed."

"Neither can I, mother. Now, lets watch this old movie and relax."

Mother cuddled beneath a throw blanket and I rested beside her.

Dr. Kyle was my first house guest. I was glad he was able to leave his practice for the week to help me get things together.

"Thank you so much, Kyle. You have no idea how much I appreciate you," I said and kissed his soft lips.

"It's my pleasure," he said as he squeezed me in a hug.

The house was beautiful. I was grateful to be able to decorate everything within the week. The house looked as if I'd been there for years instead of a week.

"There's an organic restaurant I want to take you to called Scrumptious," I said to him.

"Scrumptious, huh?" he questioned.

"Yes, and trust me, the food is absolutely scrumptious!"

"This is pretty good," Kyle said.

"I told you," I replied as I forked collard greens into my mouth.

As we were eating, Reverend Lee and Lady Laurie stopped by the table. I had no idea they were there and wished I hadn't seen them. I wondered if they saw Kyle and I playing footsie beneath the table. Kyle was also pretty tipsy.

"Kyle, this is Reverend Lee and his wife, Lady Laurie, from the church," I introduced.

Kyle wiped his mouth and hands, stood up, and greeted the them with handshakes.

Kyle's face turned a shade darker. He was embarrassed to have the pastor see him in such a state. We both were actually a little tipsy and very flirtatious at the table. I was a little embarrassed myself. I didn't know what they saw us doing.

"Well it was nice meeting you, Kyle," Lady Laurie started. "Come along dear, let's leave the love birds alone," she said with a smile.

"Yep, they saw us," I thought to myself.

Kyle and I giggled like school children at the thought of two adults being embarrassed for flirting.

Reverend Lee was at the center around ten o'clock in the morning conducting a tour for city officials. He waved when he walked past my office. I waived back and continued on with my care plans.

Reverend Lee stopped by the office when the tour was over. "Hey Camille," he said as he peeked into my office.

"Hey Reverend. How's it going?"

"It's going well. I didn't want to bother you, but Councilman Jackson, the taller gentleman with the dark blue suit was asking about you," he said.

"Asking about me?" I asked.

"Yes. He wanted to know if you were married. He left his business card."

Reverend Lee handed me the card and I looked at it for a second then put it down on the desk.

"I didn't know what to tell him after seeing you with your friend Kyle yesterday."

"How much did you see, Reverend?" I was so embarrassed.

"I don't judge. You two just looked like quite a pair. It's obvious there's history there," he said.

"Yeah, Kyle's a really good friend," and I left it at that.

He was silent for a moment. I guess he realized that I was not about to share my business with him.

"Lady Laurie and I want to come over to do you house blessing soon. We offer this service to all of our employees and church members. We do the blessing separate from the house warming," he said.

"Well that's really nice, thank you. I'll pick a date and get back to you and Lady Laurie, if that's ok."

"Now is the perfect time to have the house blessed after all the freaky things Kyle and I did when he was here," I thought to myself.

"Sounds good. Let me know," he said as he walked out of my office.

I selected April 10th at six o'clock in the evening as the day for the house blessing. I had never had a house blessing so I wasn't really sure what to expect. I did want mother to be a part of it since it's her pastor and his wife, but she had an usher board meeting that night.

The doorbell rang promptly at 6pm and I was glad because I wanted to get this over with so I could rest. I opened the door and Reverend Lee's cologne entered my nose.

"Damn he smelled good," I thought to myself. "Where is Lady Laurie," I asked him.

"She'll be her shortly. She had to address the usher board at tonight's meeting."

"Oh ok. Well I made some refreshments," I said.

"Did you? What's on the menu?" he said jokingly.

"I have my famous iced tea, curry chicken salad, and a pineapple upside down cheesecake. I bought the cheesecake from Scrumptious. I think I'm hooked," I said with a laugh.

"Yeah, that would be easy with their cooking," he replied with a laugh.

"How long do you think it will be before Lady Laurie arrives? I really don't want to start eating without her."

"Maybe another twenty or thirty minutes. Why? Is something wrong?"

"I'm a little hungry," I replied.

"Then eat! Lady Laurie won't mind at all. I promise."

"Well that's good to know!"

Reverend Lee and I washed our hands and I made the plates. He took my hand to bless the food and my body was set aflame.

"Where the hell is Lady Laurie?" I asked myself.

We sat and talked for a bit and were done before we realized that we'd been waiting for almost forty minutes.

"You want to call and check on Lady Laurie?" I asked.

"Sure, I'm going to get some more tea. May I pour you a glass?" he asked politely.

"Yes, thank you."

He returned with our glasses and I took a few swallows.

"She's on her way," he said as he drank his tea with his eyes on me.

"Great. I can't wait to dig into this cheesecake," I said to break up the tension that clearly existed between us.

The tea seemed sweeter than I remembered, but it wasn't bad. I was getting warm so I stood to turn on the ceiling fan then felt really dizzy. I caught myself on the table and Reverend Lee stood up to guide me to a chair.

"Are you ok?" he asked.

"I'm fine... or maybe I'm not. I don't know what's happening."

Reverend Lee guided me to the sofa and helped me to sit down. I held my head in hopes that it would stop spinning and then looked up at Reverend Lee.

"Thank you again," I started, and Reverend Lee pressed his lips against mine.

He was a potential MPR candidate, but I didn't want it to go down like this. I attempted to stop him, but I was weak and seeing double.

"Oh my goodness," I thought to myself. I looked at Reverend Lee, "You put something in my drink."

"Stop fighting me Camille. You've been staring at me since the day we met. You knew I was watching you in the restaurant when you were with your boy toy Kyle and you were teasing me while you were with him. I caught the hint. Lady Laurie isn't coming. We have all night. She thinks I'm going to the cigar bar after the blessing."

"I don't want you. Get off of me," I said groggily.

"No woman rejects me! You're the only one playing hard to get! Not anymore. I knew you'd be a tease that's why I put the 'sweetener' in your drink. To sweeten up the fight."

Reverend Lee raped me over and over again.

I woke up on the sofa naked. All of my clothes were on floor. I went upstairs to put on my robe and I stared at myself in the mirror.

"What the hell happened last night?"

I went back downstairs to the kitchen and everything was clean. There was evidence of a meal being cooked because the dishes had been washed, but I couldn't remember anything. I only knew my lady parts were very sore. "Oh my goodness," the memories flooded my mind like a water dam had just ruptured. "Reverend Lee raped me."

That explained everything. The women in the transitional center were staring at me because I was the new competition. They were all sleeping with him. Lady Laurie came to the job to apologize about missing the blessing.

"So how was it?" she asked.

"How was what?!" I asked defensively.

She had a confused look on her face. "The blessing, dear. How was the blessing?"

"Oh, it was ok."

"My husband loves house blessings. He usually does them alone, but since your mother is such an amazing woman, I wanted to be there as well," she said with a smile.

"I bet he does like doing them alone! HE'S A RAPIST!" I wanted to scream the truth, but simply answered with, "Yeah."

I felt so weak and helpless.

"Well the house is blessed, but we have to schedule a night where he and I come over for dinner," she said.

"Sure, we'll get something on the books soon." I said with a weak smile while thinking, "Like hell. Your husband will never see the inside of my house again. Bastard."

Weeks had passed. I continued on at work, but I stopped going to church. Mother was concerned, but I didn't care. I couldn't tell her about her beloved Pastor Lee, the rapist. I had to tell someone, but I didn't have anyone. Janine was friends with Lady Laurie and I didn't trust the snakes in the center.

Despite Kyle being an on the MPR list, he was my friend. I told him and he wanted to wring the reverend's neck. On top of all of that, my period was late. Kyle and I had sex days before the attack, but we used condoms. Kyle tried to comfort me by telling me that I could be late from the stress. A pregnancy test confirmed that I was, in fact, pregnant. I knew it was Reverend Lee's baby. I couldn't believe I was pregnant by such an awful man.

"I'm here for you, Cammie."

"I don't want you to pity me, Kyle," I said to him.

"I don't. Don't you know that I love you?" he asked.

"I guess I never really thought about it," I replied.

I was sad and Kyle could tell.

"You know, you don't have to go through with this pregnancy Camille."

"I can't stomach an abortion, Kyle."

"I understand... I think. I don't know. Just know I'm here for you."

Kyle and I were married before the baby, Kylie, was born. He moved to Memphis and opened a new practice. It was a rough start, but things smoothed out and I got used to being a wife and mother. It wasn't as bad as I thought it would be. I feared that Kyle would only see me as the woman he was screwing, but he really did love me.

Two years later, I was working as a nurse practitioner at his office and I became pregnant with my second child – the first with me and Kyle. We named him Kyle, Jr. Kyle was a great father. He loved Kylie and Kyle and treated Kylie as his own. No one knew the truth but me and him. I'm sure Reverend Lee knew, but I was no longer attending that church and no longer working for his sadistic center with those silly females.

Mother loved having her family near her. She spent so much time running behind the children that we usually had to tell her to slow it down. The children were a type of therapy for her so we welcomed it.

Mother and I sat on my patio talking one day and she told me that one of the new congregants stormed into service and accused Reverend Lee of fathering her child. Reverend Lee made a show of it. He stood in the pulpit and prayed for her "poor, misguided soul" and she was pulled out by emergency medical technicians who thought she had lost her mind. I just shook my head.

"Can you believe that Cammie?"

"I sure can," I replied as I sipped my tea.

Mother gave me a weird look, but didn't ask any questions.

"Come to find out," she continued, "he's been messing around with other women in the church, but he was paying them off. They all worked for one of the church companies and was being paid these big salaries to keep quiet."

I remained quiet and Kylie came running out on the porch. I smiled at my little girl and thanked God that she looked just like me and not that snake of a reverend.

Mother continued.

"All of this craziness sent poor Lady Laurie over the edge."

"How so?" I asked.

"You don't read the papers, watch the news Pumpkin?"

"Not with these two babies running around here," I said with a giggle.

Lady Laurie shot Reverend Lee and he's paralyzed from the neck down. What's that called again?" she asked.

"He's a quadriplegic," I said with a smile. "He'll live. We all have to live through some things. He's lucky he's not dead."

CHAPTER 13
FAKE ASS BROTHER'S ID (FBI)

"God, I hate my job," Anya said and rolled her eyes. "It's so stressful," she thought to herself as she parked her car in the lot of Willow Brook Mall. It was time to ease the stresses of the work week with some retail therapy.

Anya was an Executive Assistant at the Prudential Center. It was a good job; well-paying, and in the center of everything downtown Newark, but it was exhausting. Sometimes she just wanted to quit, but who would pay her bills and finance her lifestyle? She had recently relocated from Gloucester, Virginia hoping to find Mr. Right and live a comfortable, housewife life, but things weren't working out the way she expected. Virginia was slow, almost country-like. In New Jersey, it was almost always go, go, go and that included the men. Everyone was always too busy!

Anya looked at her watch and noted the time as six o'clock. The mall closed at nine. She had three whole hours to tear the mall up and relieve this tension. She entered the mall through Bloomingdales and a smiled instantly found its way to her face. She spent nine-hundred dollars in Bloomingdales, six-hundred in Lord & Taylor, one-hundred in MAC, and two-hundred in Victoria's Secret. The tension was gone and Anya was content.

"Ahhh…" she said as she walked through Bloomingdales to exit the mall with a smile on her face.

Anya went to push the door when a handsome stranger rushed to the door to open it for her. He caught her off guard.

"Oh, thank you," she said as she stared into his beautiful dark brown eyes.

"You're welcome," he said flashing a set of perfect white teeth.

Anya turned around and watched as he walked in the opposite direction with six bags from Bloomingdales and another from Lord & Taylor. He turned and looked back at Anya and smiled. Both continued on to their vehicles.

"Damn! I should have said something to him," Anya said out loud.

"Broke men can't shop in Bloomie's," she said to herself, "he's got some money." She started the car and sat in the car beating herself up about not speaking to him. She checked her mirrors and was ready to back out when she realized she needed gas. Anya sighed.

"I was fine! I was fine after my mini shopping spree! I blew it with Mr. Money Bags and now I need gas," Anya sighed and drove to the nearest gas station.

Anya pulled into the service station and waited for the attendant. He was taking too long so she got out the vehicle and walked into the mini-mart. As she returned to the car, she saw a gray Porche' parked behind her car. The stranger from the mall was leaning against the car using his cell phone. He turned, made eye contact with Anya and flashed those teeth.

"You following me?" she asked with a smile.

"Actually, I am," he said and ended his call.

The attendant turned to Anya and she told him to fill up her tank and gave him her credit card. "07050," she said before he asked for her zip code.

"What's your name?" he asked.

"Anya. Yours?"

"I'm Bryce," he said as he licked those pretty lips.

Anya now had a chance to look at him from head to toe. Bryce was clean and with that five-foot, ten-inch slim build that man knew how to hang a suit. He had on a tailored navy-blue suit, a light blue button-down shirt, a yellow neck tie with blue paisley prints, a solid yellow pocket square, a black belt, and black shoes.

"Damn!" Anya thought to herself, "he is clean!"

"Nice to meet you, Anya," he said.

"It's nice to meet you also," she answered.

Bryce went to speak again and his cell phone rang.

"Excuse me," he said and turned his back to her.

Anya was now able to check him out from behind. Her thoughts were interrupted when the attendant handed her back her credit card and told her she was good to go.

Bryce returned and apologized once again. But again, before he could start speaking, his cell phone rang. Anya giggled.

"I'm really sorry," he said, "it's work."

Bryce handed Anya his business card and whispered, "Call me," close to her ear.

Anya felt chills run down her spine. She took the card, smiled, and got into her car. As soon as she made it to the first parking lot, she stopped the car and looked that the business card.

"He's a lawyer!?" she said out loud. "Yes! There is a God and he heard my housewife prayer!"

Anya was looking forward to calling Bryce as soon as appropriate.

Anya was nervous. For the first time in a long time, she was uncertain with how to handle a man. She paced and questioned herself all weekend. A lawyer. She knew he was smart and sharp and she didn't want to mess this up. Anya allowed her anxiety to send her thoughts into overdrive. On Saturday she convinced herself not to call him because he was winding down from the week and probably hanging out with his family. Saturday night he was hanging out with his friends. On Sunday he was golfing, having brunch with other lawyers, or watching football all day.

Anya woke up on Monday and practically ran to work to share the news of Bryce with her coworker and friend, Candy.

"Hey girl," Candy greeted her.

Not wanting to appear desperate, Anya played it cool.

"Hey, Candy. How was your weekend?"

"It was cool," she replied. "How was yours?"

"It was good," Anya said. "I met this lawyer at the gas station on Friday, but it was nothing," she said nonchalantly.

"A lawyer? Tell me all about him!" Candy said. "Besides, I need a lawyer."

"Why, who did you kill?" Anya asked with a laugh.

"Girl, please. I need a will drawn up. Working here at Prudential you can't help but think about life insurance and things like that," she said.

Anya nodded. She understood where Candy was coming from, but her insurance plan had a different name. "Bryce Davidson." She gave Candy Bryce's card.

"Have you spoken to him yet?" Candy asked.

"No, why?"

"I'm not calling him first! That's your man!" Candy said.

Anya laughed. "Bingo!" she thought to herself. "A reason to call him."

Anya went to her office, cleared her throat, and dialed his number.

"This is Bryce," he answered.

"Hey, Bryce," she started, "this is Anya. We met..."

"At the gas station," he interrupted. "I was starting to think I wasn't going to hear from you," he said.

"Were you looking forward to hearing from me?" she asked.

"I was. I kept my phone next to me all weekend," he said.

Anya giggled.

"I can't talk long, but I wanted to tell you that my coworker, my friend, wants a will drawn up," she said.

"Sure, but only if you'll go out with me," Bryce said to her. "Where would you like to go?"

Anya was on cloud nine. "Well, I'm not from New Jersey so I'm not sure where to go," she said.

They talked a while longer about their hometowns and jobs then made plans to go to dinner in New York City the following Saturday.

Anya was enjoying her time with Bryce. They talked a lot about life and relationships and he showed her the sites of New Jersey and New York. Anya and Bryce were dating for almost two weeks when she reminded him about Candy's will. He called and left her a voice message to schedule an appointment.

Anya was ecstatic. She was loving the fact that she was spending time with this rich lawyer, but was also starting to like him a lot. After about a month, she decided it was time to take their relationship to the next level.

Friday arrived and Anya told Candy about her weekend plans.

"What you got planned for the weekend?" Candy asked.

"Bryce and I are hanging out," she said with a smile.

"Oh, that's cool. Can you please ask him to call me. I understand he's busy and all, but I really want to get my will done. I want him to do it, but if he's too busy I'll have to find someone else," Candy said.

"Well did you call him back when he called you the first time?" Anya asked defensively.

Candy caught the defensive attitude and dismissed it. "He never called me Anya. I called him twice and he hasn't returned my call."

"I was there when he called you, Candy. I heard him leave the voice message," Anya replied, still in defensive mode.

Frustrated with Anya's attitude, Candy crossed her arms and asked, "Did you see him dial the number?"

She didn't. She only heard him say the words.

"Well I'll talk to him about it when I see him tomorrow," Anya said.

"Thank you," Candy said, "and make sure you get a manicure before your date," she said with a playful laugh.

Anya laughed, but was still a little disturbed that Candy implied Bryce lied about the call and that she called her out about her nails – even though she was right.

Anya wanted the night to be special so she went shopping at The Mall at Short Hills. As Anya drove through Millburn on her way to the mall, she looked at the beautiful homes and thought about where she and Bryce would live after they were married. She knew he lived in a nice area, but she wasn't sure if he would want to move someplace else when they decided to start a family

Anya arrived at the mall on a mission. She knew she wanted something black, tight, sexy, and simple for the night. She bought a black cocktail dress from Nordstrom and strappy, open-toe shoes from Christian Louboutin. She left the mall and went to the nail salon for a mani-pedi and to have her eyebrows waxed. Anya was ready for the night.

Bryce called Anya to see if she was ready for their date.

"Hey B," she answered.

Bryce laughed. "Hey, you ready?" he asked.

"I sure am," she answered. "I like surprises, but I have to admit, I'm a little nervous," she said.

"Do you trust me, baby?" he asked.

"I do," she answered softly.

"Then don't be nervous," he said. "I'll be there in thirty minutes."

"Ok," she answered with a smile and they ended the call.

Bryce met Anya at her door when he picked her up for their date. She was nervous and excited at the same time. He took her to a glass-enclosed rooftop restaurant in New York and Anya was amazed.

"I'm going to marry this man," she thought to herself as she looked around.

Bryce and Anya spent the evening joking, laughing, and sharing stories about life until it was time to leave. Anya was full from food and fun and she was now ready for a release. Bryce pulled up to his house in Livingston. Anya tried hard not to stop and stare, but couldn't help herself.

"Wow," she said

"What's the matter?" Bryce said as he took her by the hand.

"Your house is beautiful."

"Why thank you," he started, "I kind of like it myself," he said with a chuckle.

Anya smiled and let him escort her into the house.

On the way into the house Anya asked about Candy.

"B, I know you've been busy, but did Candy ever call you back about drawing up her will?"

"Who?" he asked.

That kind of shocked Anya. "Candy, my co-worker."

"Oh, no," he started, "she never called me back."

Anya didn't know Candy to lie, but she stopped thinking about it because she wanted to enjoy her evening with Bryce. "Ok, she answered."

Anya entered the house and was amazed.

"Your home is beautiful," she exclaimed. "Do you shop at Lugano's?" she asked.

Bryce chuckled. "Look at you," he said. "What you know about Lugano's?"

"I know I love their furniture, but I have an Ashley Furniture budget," she said.

They shared a laugh and he invited her to the bedroom. She wanted to stay in the living room to enjoy the furniture and cuddle with him, by the fire, but it was evident that dinner put him in the mood. His bedroom furniture was equally beautiful. Beside the luxe furniture, Anya was also seeing dollar signs.

Bryce turned on some jazz and invited Anya to dance.

"I could grow to love this," Anya thought to herself as she looked up into Bryce's eyes.

"What are you thinking about?" he asked her.

Boldly, she answered, "What you'll feel like inside of me."

Bryce smiled and kissed Anya softly before leading her to his bed.

Bryce was everything Anya had imagined. She hoped for forty-five minutes to an hour, but settled for the fifteen in hopes of a round two. Bryce got up to get a glass of wine for him and Anya and she realized that his cell phone kept vibrating. He was gone for quite some time when his house phone started ringing. The phone easily rang ten times.

"Your phones keep ringing," Anya said when he returned.

"Thanks," he said and handed her the glass.

"Is everything ok at work?" she asked as he looked through his phone.

"That's agent life for you," he said.

"Agent life?" Anya asked.

"Yeah, when you're an FBI agent your life doesn't really belong to you anymore," he said.

"Ummm… you told me you were a lawyer," Anya said.

"I never told you that," he said with a straight face.

"Maybe I thought you said that," she said and watched his demeanor which never changed.

"I didn't *think* anything," Anya thought to herself. "Why would Candy need her will drawn up by an FBI agent?!"

"You ready for round two?" Bryce said with a smile and leaned towards Anya.

"Um, you kind of wore me out the first round. I think I'm going to go home, shower, and rest up for next time," she said with smile.

"Ok, let me get dressed, I'll take you home," he said.

"No, it's fine," she said. "I'll grab a taxi and call you when I get home."

Bryce didn't like that idea, but he agreed and Anya left.

Monday arrived and Candy met Anya at the elevator.

"Good morning," Anya said with a confused look on her face.

"Good morning, your boy is a fraud!" Candy said seriously.

"What are you talking about?" Anya asked.

"I started doing some research on Bryce…" she started.

"Research? Why are you researching my boyfriend?" Anya said as she dropped her things on her desk.

"Because his actions were suspect," she answered.

Anya knew Candy was right and she gave in.

"What did you find?" she whispered.

"He is not a lawyer. Bryce Davidson does not even exist!" she exclaimed.

"What?!" Anya said.

"Girl, sit!"

Anya sat down and let Candy talk.

"I was making calls last night and my sister, Natalia, overhead me say his name. She told me that she knew him. Long story short, he's a liar.

He is a con man girl! He got over on my sister using the name Wynton Davidson saying he was an FBI agent. Natalia wants you to call her so she can give you all of the details."

Candy's phone started to ring and she had to leave Anya.

Anya sat in silence all day. She couldn't believe this was happening to her. No wedding. No house in Livingston. No gray Porche'.

Anya called Natalia immediately after work.

"Anya, hey, Candy told me about your run-in with Wynton. Well, what did he tell you his name was?"

"Bryce," Anya said in disbelief. "He told me his name was Bryce."

"Sis, after I learned what I could about him, I learned that he goes by Wynton, MJ, Adrian, Luther and another name I can't remember. He took me to this beautiful house in Livingston, but I later found out that was his mother's house. He pretends its his to impress women. Girl, he lied about being an agent for the FBI, DEA, a lawyer, and a real estate broker. His ass is unemployed!" Natalia said with a laugh. "I can't believe he's still pulling this shit on women. Ridiculous. Did you get the five minutes of fame?" she asked.

"Five minutes of fame?" Anya finally spoke.

"Yes, girl he's a two-minute brother. It was more like fifteen minutes, but you know what I mean," Natalia said.

"Um," Anya was dumbfounded.

"Well, if you did, I hope you used a condom because he is a whore. He's slept with women all up and down the east coast," Natalia finished.

"Natalia," Anya interrupted, "I've heard enough."

"No problem, girl," she started, "have a good night." Natalia was still laughing when the call ended.

Anya had thought about everything that took place from the very beginning and couldn't help but to bust out laughing. This was her own fault for being a gold digger. I let a well-known dog and con man run his weak game on me. Next time, I'll listen to the words of mom, "Everything that glitters isn't gold."

CHAPTER 14
OFFICER BUT NOT A GENTLEMAN

I swear I don't know how I get myself into these situations. I was boy crazy when I was a teenager; maybe it just never wore off. In any case, I've always been drawn to military men. There was something about a man in a uniform that just made my mouth water. It didn't matter it if was Navy, Army, Marine, Air Force, Coast Guard... hell, even a man in policeman's uniform got me hot and bothered. This is what caused my current state of affairs.

I remember the day I met Omar Richards. He was at a local lounge with a few other officers. He was sitting at the bar and I remember sitting across the bar making eyes at him. He wanted me to think he was shy. He smiled and would turn his head a bit, but he always turned back to look at me and I was looking right back at him. I am not the shy type and I wasn't going to pretend to be. I sent a drink over to him with my phone number and he walked over to meet me.

I watched him as he walked over in that uniform and sipped my drink as I sized him up. Omar was six feet tall and had an athletic build. His uniform was loose fitting, but I could see the definition of his chest and arms through his uniform. Omar was handsome. He was fair-skinned, and had hazel eyes. He had bright pink lips that hid cute, crooked teeth within his boyish smile.

"Thanks for the drink, Candice," he said to me.

"You're very welcome, sir," I said seductively.

Omar smiled.

"You know my name, but I don't know yours."

"My name is Omar, Candice," he said shyly. He had an accent, but I couldn't tell where he was from.

157

"Officer Omar," I said as I ran my fingers down the front of his shirt.

"Where are you from?" I asked him.

"Atlanta," he answered.

I couldn't help but laugh because you could hear it even more now. Uniform and an accent? It was definitely time to go.

"Did you drive here?" I asked him.

"No, I rode with the boys," he said and smiled.

I stood up and placed my hands on his thighs. "Let me take you home," I said.

He looked at me as if it were more of a question. It was a statement, though. I wanted to know if what I felt was in his pocket or in his pants.

The twenty-minute ride home was filled with pointless banter. Then he told me that he had been in the Army for 11 years and was in charge of weapons coordination and distribution. All I heard was "job security"! Thoughts of the rest of the evening danced around in my mind and I put the pedal to the metal to get the fantasy started. I put the key in the door and almost ripped Omar's uniform off of his body. I hadn't enjoyed myself that much in over a year. Omar was definitely a keeper.

Omar and I were kicking it for two weeks. He was sexy and the sex was outstanding. I thought this was going to be a one-nighter, but it turned into a two-weeker and I was in love! I had literally started planning our wedding. We were getting married and having a reception on a Spirit of Norfolk cruise and were honeymooning in Hawaii after he returns from his deployment. I was ready! My friends and I were out ring shopping and I was waiting for Omar to pop the question. Of course, Omar and I had never discussed marriage, but that was beside the point.

I thought we were going to take it to the next level by the end of the following month, but Omar changed and things came to a screeching halt. He'd cut back on the phone and booty calls. I was done! I tried calling him for two weeks, but was never able to reach him. I was pissed off!

I had my friends on the prowl.

"Girl, if you see him, call me!" My friends thought I was crazy. I may have been a little off, but I was serious.

Omar called me about three weeks later and gave me some BS story about a secret mission. He told me that General Schwarzkopf called him on a secret mission and he was deployed without notice. I could not believe he wanted me to believe that the same General Schwarzkopf of Operation Desert Storm had called him personally for a mission. He must have thought I was stupid to believe that nonsense. I was stupid for him for a while, but not anymore. It didn't take too much investigating to cold bust his black ass. Not only was he playing me, but he had a woman in Norfolk and another in Virginia Beach. I should have known that pretty boy was a player. He was only pretending to be shy.

I probably should have just walked away and let the whole thing go, but I wanted revenge. Omar was infatuated with his cherry red BMW. He almost never drove it and he kept it garaged except for when he was out on the town. The girls and I plotted to key his car and flatten his tires. It was full proof! We executed the plan and sat outside waiting for him to come out to meet every scratch from the front to the back of the vehicle.

We were sitting in my car waiting for him to come out when the military police pulled up and knocked on his door.

"Ooh girl, what's going on?" one of my friends asked.

"Shh," I hushed her.

I couldn't hear what had happened, but Omar was escorted out in handcuffs.

Two days later I was reading the Daily Press and saw that he was arrested for stealing government furniture.

"Stealing furniture?! Who the hell does that!?" I said out loud.

Needless to say, he was going to jail. I didn't really get my revenge because he never saw the car, but I was glad to know he wasn't getting away with his foolishness.

"Here's a middle finger salute to you, officer" I said as I closed the paper.

CHAPTER 15
GOOD TO ME BUT NOT GOOD FOR ME

"State your name for the record," the officer said.

"Payton Wright," she answered sadly.

"Do you know why you're here, Payton," he asked.

"Yes," she answered with tears now streaming down her face.

"Why are you here?"

Payton wiped her eyes and nose with her sleeve, but remained silent.

The officer waited.

"Payton," he said.

Payton looked at the officer with wet eyes.

"Why are you here?" he repeated.

"Because of Braeden," she whispered.

"Right," the officer said. "Are you sure you don't want a lawyer?"

"I'm sure," she said. "I'm innocent and I don't have anything to hide."

The officer handed Payton an attorney waiver and an ink pen. She signed the form and handed it back to the officer.

"You don't want to read it?" he asked.

"Like I said, I'm innocent," she answered.

He placed it in a folder in front of himself and leaned forward on the table. "Now," he started, "Tell me what happened in your own words. Start at the beginning."

Payton took a deep breath, looked into the camera then off to the floor as she began to speak.

"Braeden and I were together for three years," she said. "It's obvious," she said and looked around the interrogation room, "that he was good to me, but not so good for me. Braeden sold a lot of drugs. He was a big-time dealer."

"Was he carrying weight the entire time?" the officer interrupted.

Payton dropped her head and answered, "Yes."

"Continue," the officer said.

"Braeden wasn't a bad guy."

The officer giggled.

"What's so funny?" Payton asked defensively.

"He wasn't a bad guy, but you're here and he's in the wind," the officer replied. "He's not even thinking about you."

Payton continued with her story. "I felt like a first grader when we were together. I used to scribble 'Payton loves Braeden' on pieces of paper and napkins. We went out to dinner all the time and each restaurant was a new adventure for me. The five-star restaurants in Miami were the highlights of our week because I had never experienced such dining delights. I was his escort at social mixers and upscale parties he was invited to. We had courtside seats for all of the Miami Heat games. Braeden was a celebrity in his own right. He had so many invitations to events that I couldn't keep up. Between general social parties and the parties with his crew I spent more time shopping for the right outfit than anything else. He even bought me a fur coat," she said with a giggle. "No one needs a fur coat in Miami," she said and looked off with a smile.

"What activities went on at the parties with his crew?"

"Nothing much," she shrugged. "They drank, smoked cigars, smoked marijuana sometimes, gambled, played cards. That was pretty much it," she answered.

"When you met Braeden, what did he tell you he did for a living?"

Payton shrugged, "he didn't. I never asked," she answered.

The officer shook his head. "Continue," he said.

"You have to understand," officer. "Braeden grew up really poor. He was happiest in his life when he was doing nice things for other people and he was always doing nice things for me. He made his mistakes, but he wasn't a bad guy," she pleaded.

"Need I remind you that you're in custody and he hasn't returned any of your phone calls."

"I know, but he could have spent all of his money on himself. Instead he wore sneakers, t-shirts, and jeans. He only purchased nice clothes when he attended the celebrity events. He even bought his family a beautiful home in Mount Dora," she said.

The officer started writing in his notebook and Payton stopped speaking.

"Continue," he said.

"So, like I was saying, they have a beautiful home in Mount Dora and he took me out to visit them a few times."

"Who is them?" the officer asked.

"Huh?" Payton asked confused.

"You said he took you out to visit 'them' when you went to Mount Dora. Who lives in Mount Dora?"

"Oh, his mother and his two sisters. His wife and children live near there, but I don't know where," she replied.

The officer sat back and allowed Payton to tell way more than he'd asked.

"So he's married?"

"Yes," she started, "well, they've been going through a divorce for the last six years. When..."

"Six years?" the officer interrupted.

"Yes, but that's only because there are kids involved. When kids are involved it can be kind of hard," she said firmly.

"How old are his children?"

"Ramona will be seventeen this year and Tyler will be sixteen this year," she said.

The officer stared at her. He didn't know if Payton was really this dense or if she was trying to bury Braeden. He settled on her being stupid and just allowed her to keep talking.

"Braeden opens up his home to those in need, but they had to be close friends. When he bought my condo, he was strict about who could come stay with us. He didn't care about the Mini Cooper," she said with a giggle. "Not having to worry about living expenses and transportation allowed me to complete my degree in Social Work."

"Are you telling me that the condo you live in and the car you are driving right now was purchased by Braeden?" the officer asked directly.

Payton hesitated, but then answered. "Yes, but his name isn't on the condo or the car. Just me and mama's name is on the house and the car is in my name," she insisted.

"That's fine," he answered and scribbled in his notebook. "Continue."

"He only bought the car because my Toyota Camry conked out on me last year. And that's what I mean when I said he was good to me, but not good for me. He did a lot of things for me, but I knew dating a drug dealer wasn't the safest or the smartest, but I loved him."

The officer looked at Payton blankly.

"Have you ever had any interactions with his wife?"

Payton rolled her eyes. "More than I wanted to. There were countless times when she stopped me in the street to fight me! Can you believe that?" Payton asked seriously.

The officer chuckled but didn't respond.

"His kids hate me because of what she told them about me."

"What do you think she told them?" he asked.

"That I ruined their family. I didn't break up his family though. I didn't even know he was married until I asked him if he thought he would ever be interested in marrying me. He said, 'I already got a wife' but then he stopped like what he said had slipped. I went off! That's when he told me they were in the process of a divorce. He also said she didn't like the fact that he was buying me things."

"Were you ever afraid of his wife?"

"Hell no! I know how to handle my own. I was more concerned about his 'occupation' and if I would get caught in the middle."

"Why? Did something happen?"

"We were leaving a Heat game one night. We got to his car and there was a hole in the windshield."

"What kind of hole?"

"It was from a gunshot?" she answered.

"How do you know it was from a gunshot?" he asked.

"Braeden told me. I guess he had seen something similar," she shrugged. "I don't know. I only know that I was nervous. I knew I should have left him alone then, but I didn't. I kind of couldn't." Payton paused.

"Why? Were you afraid of him?"

"No, never!" she exclaimed.

Payton paused again. The officer waited.

"You ever heard that song called 'Gotta Leave You Alone'?" she asked.

"Can't say that I have," he answered.

"You must have. It's by Jeezy and it features Neyo."

The officer continued to stare at her with no further response about the song.

"Well anyway, in the song, this girl falls for this hustler and in the song she actually says, something like, 'You ain't no good, but you feel so good... something, something, something, I know you're bad, but I want you so bad.' That's how it felt. I knew he wasn't good for me, but I wanted him so badly."

"Continue on with the story, Ms. Wright," the officer said.

"After the craziness with the bullet hole in the windshield, Braeden hired a full-time security guard named Doc. He was big – muscular," she said as she widened her arms to mimic the girth of Doc's body, "bald, and quiet. And he carried a gun," she added. "The true definition of strong, silent type. Him being around made me feel a lot better; a lot less nervous."

"What was the guard's name?" he asked.

"Doc," she answered.

"His real name."

"Oh, I don't know. Like I said, he was quiet. But he followed us everywhere we went. I told my mother about the situation after the game and she was worried. I assured her that everything would be fine. I had Braeden, we had Doc, and I carried my own protection," she said.

"We confiscated your nine-millimeter," the officer said.

"You what? How? It wasn't in the car when I was stopped; it was at home," she said.

"I know. We searched your home during this investigation."

"Will I get it back?" she asked.

"Probably not."

Payton was quiet.

"What was your relationship like with Braeden?"

"It was great. We were in love," Payton paused.

"Something else to add about relationship?" the officer asked.

"Well, I later found out that Braeden was cheating on me with that crazy bitch, Tamara. I mean, I felt like there was someone else, but could never prove it.

"Tell me about it," the officer said.

"I was his number one," she said. "I had full access to properties, cars, everything."

The officer scribbled some more into his notebook.

"I mean, I would always see other females around him, but they knew who I was."

"What do you mean?"

"On the days I would show up for his parties I would see different women sitting beside him or standing beside him. They would sometimes give me dirty looks. I guess they were hoping I wouldn't show up so they could make their move on him, but they would always step off when they saw me. Everyone knew who I was; they even referred to me as Ms. Brae."

"How did you find out about Tamara?"

"I asked him," she said.

"And he told you the truth?"

"No," she said and rolled her eyes. "He lied. He said she was the money maid."

"The money maid?" he asked.

"Yeah, she counted his money," she said and rolled her eyes again.

"You were jealous," the officer said with a smile.

"I just didn't like how she was always hanging around my man."

The officer giggled.

"You know that rap artist, Nicki Minaj, right? Well, that's how she was shaped and she wore things that accentuated her perfect breasts, small waist, and big ol' booty. I mean, I'm no slouch. I look good, but her ass draws a lot more attention."

The officer laughed out loud.

"I was hating, but I tried not to show it. I couldn't understand how it was that she had earned Braeden's trust to the point where she was counting his money. I knew where he kept it and he gave me money all the time, but she had access codes, PINs, and combinations to locks. I asked Braeden if he was having sex with her or if he ever had and he said no. He never lied to me, so I didn't have any reason not to believe him. Anyway, enough about her. Can I have something to eat?"

"What do you want?"

"I don't know," she said and looked up to the ceiling.

The officer rolled his eyes. "How about a burger and some fries?"

"How about a steak, a sweet potato, a side of steamed broccoli with melted cheese, and a glass of wine?" she said with a sly smile.

"You can have everything but the wine," he said.

"No problem," she said with the smile of a small child.

The officer returned with a hamburger, sweet potato fries, raw broccoli with a side of ranch dressing, and a grape soda. He handed the tray to Payton and sat at the table across from her. Payton stared at the food, sighed, and ate a fry.

"Ok, Payton," the officer started, "I've heard enough about parties, property, and Nicki Minaj. Tell me about the shooting."

Payton took a deep breath and rubbed her injured shoulder. "Braeden and I were supposed to be having dinner at a new restaurant. I was out shopping when he called and told me that he was running late."

"Did he say why?" the officer asked.

Payton shrugged. "He only said he had some unfinished business to take care of and said he would meet me at the restaurant."

The officer nodded.

"Braeden was almost an hour late. I was upset because I don't like when he makes me wait for business, but he was jittery when he arrived. He was looking around a lot and shifting in his seat. I asked if he was ok. He took hold of my hand and said, 'Yeah, sweetheart, my situation just got pretty intense.' That made me a nervous because I'd never seen him nervous before. I looked around and saw Doc and two other big guys. 'Who are those guys with Doc?' I asked him. 'Don't worry,' Braeden said to me with a smile. 'So why are they here?' I asked him. 'Even Doc needs a vacation,' he said with a laugh. We ordered dinner and he asked me to come over. I told him I had to take my mother to a doctor's appointment, but would see him afterwards. We finished our meal and Doc escorted me home that night. After my mother's appointment I went over to Braeden's house."

Payton's eyes dropped to the table and she became silent. The officer could see she was becoming upset, but he didn't say anything.

Payton took a deep breath and continued. "I was always excited to see him. I loved him so much," she said. "I saw the bullet holes in the door before my foot hit the steps. I figured that was why Braeden was so shook the night before. Someone was after him. For the life of me, though, I couldn't understand why anyone would get mad at him. He was generous and fair. He was always doing extra for his workers, his friends, and his family. Braeden was a good man. I mean, I know the street pharmacy business can be kind of cut throat, but he was well respected," she said.

"There is a very big difference between respect and fear," the officer said to her.

Payton looked confused, but she understood. She sighed.

"I spoke to Braden about the bullet holes in the door and reminded him about the bullet holes in the car window and he assured me that everything was taken care of. 'We're safe,' he said to me, and I believed him. We stayed at his townhouse in Miami that night."

"Where is it located?" he asked generally.

Payton gave him the address.

"Ironically, I slept like a baby that night. Braeden always made me feel safe. I had class the next day so I knew I couldn't sleep in. I got up and Braeden was already gone. I wasn't afraid, but I did wonder why he left without saying anything to me. Something seemed different. I couldn't really place what it was, but something felt off. Braeden called and disturbed my thoughts. He asked me to go to Tamara's house to pick up some money. That was weird to me because he trusted me, but he never asked me to pick up money."

"Why do you think that is?" the officer asked.

"He said he never wanted me involved."

The officer stared at her. She had a college degree, but was as dumb as a doorknob when it came to this guy. "Continue," he said to her.

"He texted me Tamara's address. She lived in a beautiful, upscale neighborhood. I had to ring the doorbell twice before she answered the door. You could hear the frustration in her voice when she answered. 'Who is it?' With her nasty self. I never liked her," Payton said and rolled her eyes. "She seemed surprised when she opened the door and saw me. 'Where the hell is Braeden?' she asked. I told her he sent me and she rolled her eyes. I asked her what was with her attitude and she spilled the beans. Told me about how she was still sleeping with Braeden and she was pissed that he was making her play seconds to me. I was hot like fire! She looked at me and could tell that I didn't know and she started smiling. 'I was his girl first,' she said. 'I was surprised that after all this time he didn't move you to counting, then I realized that he started giving more money to his wife, which meant he went back to her again.' I was shocked. I believed her, but I didn't want to believe her. 'What do you mean again?' Tamara laughed. She was getting a thrill out of knowing more about him than me. I felt so stupid, but I couldn't let her see it. 'Just give me the bag, bitch,' I said to her. She tossed three bags at me one by one. They were kind of heavy so I carried out the first then went back into the house for the others." Payton paused. "I egged her on," she said with a nod. "I stopped in the walkway before leaving the house after the final pick-up and told her I couldn't wait to tell Braeden everything she told me and she lost it! That crazy bitch pulled out a gun and took shots at me and one hit me in the shoulder. Thankfully it only grazed me, but it made me drop the bag. I ran out of there, jumped into my car, and pulled off. I kept calling Braeden, but he wasn't answering the phone. I didn't even realize that I was speeding. Next thing I knew, there were flashing lights in my rearview mirror. There was blood on my shirt and the steering wheel from my shoulder. That's what got me caught up in this BS; messing around with that crazy broad."

"That's not what got you caught up, Payton. What messed you up was that you got involved with a drug dealer that didn't give a damn about you. Do you even know what was in the bags you carried out of the house?"

Payton stared defiantly at the officer.

"Well, do you?" he asked seriously.

"He sent me over there for money so obviously it was money," she answered.

"Money would have been better for your case," he said as he closed his notebook.

"So what was in the bag?"

"Drugs. Twenty kilos of cocaine in one bag and thirty kilos in the other along with a few thousand dollars."

The officer watched the blood drain from Payton's face. "You still think he's a generous guy? A giving guy? He's a selfish son of a bitch! You just can't see it," the officer said sternly.

"But what about Tamara?!" she exclaimed. "She's the one who gave me the money, I mean the drugs! I thought it was money!"

"Interestingly enough," he started, "she's blaming everything on you. The money, the drugs, the shooting. She said..."

"Wait," Payton interrupted, "you have her here?" she asked.

"We do. You think you can just shoot guns in a neighborhood like that and neighbors not call the police? She said you came there and threatened and that's why she shot at you. Problem was that the neighbors had been wanting her out of the neighborhood because of the 'questionable company' she kept. We got a warrant and found money and drugs, but she said it was yours."

"Did she tell you where Braeden was?"

The officer chuckled. "Funny girl, that Tamara, she never mentioned Braeden's name. She blamed everything on you. Said you were financing and supplying everything. Other than you mentioning Braeden's name, we would have never known he existed."

Payton was in shock. "You can't possibly believe any of this! I'm innocent!" she screamed.

"You're not innocent, Payton. Naïve, but not innocent at all. You knew about everything, but you trusted Braeden so you looked the other way. And now, you're going to take the fall for all of it."

Payton was quiet.

"You have anything else you want to add?" the officer asked.

"Can I have a lawyer?"

The officer chuckled. "You want a lawyer now?"

"Yes!" she screamed. "As a matter of fact, you can't use any of what I told you against me because I didn't have a lawyer!"

The officer opened the folder and held up the waiver. "I read you your rights and offered you a lawyer. You declined. This form," he said as he shook it in front of her, "says that you are aware of your rights and that you don't want a lawyer. You're innocent. You have nothing to hide. That's what you said to me. Remember?"

"I didn't know!" she cried. "I didn't know!"

"You probably didn't know," he said as he gathered his things, "but I bet you learned today."

The officer gathered his things and left Payton crying hysterically in the interrogation room.

Tamara was sentenced to five years in prison for drug possession and assault and battery. Her sentence was lessened for testifying again Payton. She maintained that she never knew or heard of Braeden.

Payton was sentenced to ten years in prison for drug possession with the intent to distribute.

Braeden's family was questioned, but his wife hadn't seen him since the day of the incident between Tamara and Payton.

Made in USA - North Chelmsford, MA
1163497_9780578500607
09.10.2020 1750